LET GO

A Sweet Story About Letting Go
And Forgiveness.

Claudette McLennon

EXPLORA BOOKS
700 – 838 West Hastings St. Vancouver
BC V6C 0A6
www.explorabooks.com
Phone: (604) 330 6795

ISBN: 978-1-997587-36-1 (Paperback)
978-1-83430-123-5 (Hardback)
978-1-997587-37-8 (eBook)

Claudette McLennon

LET GO

A Sweet Story About *Letting Go*
And Forgiveness.

Table of Contents

Acknowledgement

I wish to thank my family for the love and support received from the start of the book to the end. Special thanks to the siblings, nieces, and nephews who coaxed me through the process. Your encouragement was the boost needed to navigate the path to completion. Moreso, gratitude to Gee, who fostered my early love for reading, and Harry for his storytelling. And to Dudley, always in my corner, and Michael, Jan, Norma, and Janet for cheering me on. And of course, thanks to the Creator for giving me the inspiration to do this.

Chapter 1

Joyce Brooks died at thirty-nine, leaving an only child, Madison Joy Brookes. Madison is seventeen and has already completed one year of college. She had been accepted at all six colleges she had applied, having carried a straight 4.0 average since she started school. Both she and her mother had been inseparable. They were best friends. Now she is hurting like hell.

She had time off from school and was offered grief counselling. There is a void so big inside her; she wonders if she can or would ever be normal again. There is numbness, and there is pain, and both wage war on her. She hates living right now. She cannot see the point. "Why my mother?" she wonders. "What evil was making her an orphan?"

She rejects the idea that her father is out there somewhere. He was quiet for seventeen years, and he better remain that—quiet. It was bad enough her mother died, but to saddle her with meeting her father and getting to know him was unfair.

Joyce met the handsome Vernal Moodie when he was recovering from surgery. She was at NYU Medical Center. He was pleasant, if slightly grumpy, but had changed as the beautiful Joyce fetched him water, kept his jug full of ice, and brought him fruits. Tired of his grumpiness, she offered to sing him a lullaby and was startled when he burst out laughing.

There was such a transformation of his features! Joyce was struck by love then.

He was seven years her senior, but it did not seem to matter. His two broken ribs seemed to heal at record speed after that. Before his discharge, he had asked her for her number, which she gladly gave. She knew he was single and was an officer on the USS *Missouri*. He was injured when a truck sideswiped him, and his car skidded off the road down an embankment. He was lucky to have only two broken ribs and a gash at his hairline above his right ear. He planned to do twenty years with the navy and then retire and operate a yacht chartering business. In addition, he would operate a ferry service from Manhattan to Fire Island.

During the time they were together, Joyce forgot much of the teachings of her parents. Her father was a lay minister and was very strict. He took his role seriously and was not shy about his children's disobedience. He was not a boisterous man, but you felt his wrath. Being grounded for two weeks was mild vacation; a month Rikers Island and three months Alcatraz.

Her brother Fitzroy had come up with the names for the sentencings, much to the amusement of her sister Carol and herself. Admonitions were more frequent for the girls and more stringent for him. Parents were always worried about teenage pregnancy and with good reason.

Joyce continued at NYU Medical Center but for less days and hours. It became a smoke screen for her meeting Verne. Her auditions for parts on Broadway were few at that time, and whereas in the past would be calling the agency she had registered with repeatedly in a week, it was now weekly. Standing at five feet six inches, even though she was talented, she knew her height had her at disadvantage.

Joyce remembered the battle with her father when she decided to become a dancer. She had used all her intelligence to point out that Broadway shows were neither sleazy nor necessarily corruptive. She had informed him that many Christians went to see the shows. Her dance teacher Ms. Johnson did her part as well.

Surprisingly, her mother backed her. She had attended Brooklyn Theatre Arts High School, which was just minutes away from home. She also attended Bernice Johnson dance school. She was proud that Ben Vereen was an alumnus. She was really tops in school, but out there were many talented dancers, and exceptional was the requirement, or lady luck had to intervene.

Now here she was, so deeply in love with this man seven years her senior. Age did not matter. They were compatible. They laughed at the same things, enjoyed the same kinds of food, and loved spy/mystery novels. They both loved to draw. Where he had real talent, she stuck to stickmen.

Madison wondered why her mother's life story intruded. She knew her heart was breaking. Her mother was her world. They had really been the best of friends. Why did she have to die? She was hurting badly.

By now, relatives, friends, and coworkers had stopped coming by. She had stayed with her grandparents after her mother died. She was not brave enough to stay by herself, even though she craved that. She wanted to wallow in her grief. She had a right to. She still did not see or understand why her mother wanted to saddle her with a father she never knew, who had never bothered to come back to her or for her mother. She snorted in disgust. Some love!

Madison sat morosely in the dark-brown chair, wishing it was black; then everything would be perfect—black mood, bleak outlook, loss of hope, and barren future! Her eyes glinted with malice as she remembered dear old Dad. She was to meet him day after tomorrow. Well, Dad, she thought to herself, you have a treat in store. How best can she offend him? Colored hair? Maybe purple or green, heavy black eyeliner, royal blue eyeshadow, and black lipstick. For the first time since her mother's death, she didn't feel comatose. It would also mean she would have to go to the hair supply store. That made her hesitate, but she decided Dad really needed a welcome, one she felt obliged to provide. She decided she would tell her lawyer Grosman to tell him she would meet at their office.

Her grandmother Ethel plied her with food. She ate some more to get rid of her. She just wasn't in the mood for food. She knew she was being ungracious, but she hoped one day she would show her gratitude as she had been taught. She vacillated between weeping and being philosophical—that everyone dies, that she had a future, and that her mother was watching over her.

On Wednesday, she went to the store to buy her apparatus for her appointment on Thursday. She got everything she needed. She declined to have her grandmother accompany her to Court Street at Grosman and Bartlett. She had her aunt Carol accompany her instead. She had all her props in a bag and arranged to meet her aunt in the lobby. She did her eyes, making her long lashes thick with mascara. The other props would be completed in the bathroom. When she met her aunt in the lobby, she told her she had to use the bathroom. Her aunt looked askance at her face.

She just shook her head and told her aunt no judgment, just to support her.

On the fifth floor, they got off, and she hurried to the bathroom. Aunt Carol came in behind her, and Maddi dutifully entered a stall, then came out. She started to complete her image. She put on a green wig, the left side cut short; black lipstick; and a ring, which she fastened on her nose. Aunt Carol's look was comical. She seemed like she wanted to cry and laugh at the same time. "What have you done to yourself?" she asked.

"Remember, no judgment! I do not want anything to do with that man. I liked him before: quiet and far away. That's the way I like it—quiet! He can go back from whence he came. That should not be too hard. He has seventeen years of practice."

Aunt Carol stood with her mouth agape. "Is that what this getup is about, to get rid of your father? Oh, my niece, be careful this doesn't hurt you instead."

"I know you mean well, Auntie C., but this is between Lieutenant, Colonel, or whatever his rank is. I will be civil," she said.

The offices of Grosman and Barlett were spacious and clean. The carpet was thick and muffled the footsteps. There were pieces of abstract art on the walls. In the waiting area, there was a portable water cooler with discreet white cups. There were about four people in the waiting room.

Soon, they were called and ushered into a smaller room. They thanked the polite receptionist and sat down. Maddi wondered idly how many people were executed in that room. They waited for the meeting to begin. Soon, the door opened, and two men walked in. One was impressive in a gray suit with a white shirt. The other was well dressed too, in a black suit and light-gray shirt, but he lacked the commanding appearance. The latter cleared his throat and addressed them. He was Shane Grosman. He then introduced Lieutenant Commander Moodie and rightly assumed her to be Madison Brookes. She thought his name was Harry Grosman, and he didn't seem that quiet when she had seen him first. He smiled and told them his brother Harry had initially contacted them, but he was away, so he was filling in. Maddi breathed a sigh of relief. She was not imagining things. Mr. Grosman greeted Aunt Carol after asking her name.

He explained that her mother had contacted him to carry out some last request. However, he would give the parties ten minutes to introduce themselves. He hurriedly left the room. Mr. Moodie was clearly as uncomfortable as she was. He addressed Madison, expressing his condolences for the loss of her mother and wishing he had met Madison under more pleasant circumstances. He was sorry for his absence over the years but never knew he had a daughter and was hoping to get to know her.

Maddi stared at him, and it was only with Aunt Carol's jab in the side that she nodded in acknowledgment. She thanked him for his expression of sympathy and told him she was fine living with her grandparents. There was no further need for his service. She could see traces of red cross his cheeks and the flare of his nose. Bull's-eye, she thought maliciously. The barb had hit like she planned. They looked at each other, two adversaries! He did not scare her. He should go back home or to the navy; she didn't care which.

Shane Grosman returned looking pleased and said he would disclose her mother's will and last request. Her mother had an insurance policy of 250,000 dollars. The bulk of her estate belonged to her only child; 150,000 dollars in personal effects, except for a tennis bracelet with a matching chain that went to her sister Carol and a pearl necklace for her mother. Her siblings were to inherit thirty thousand while the parents twenty thousand each. Maddi was surprised and perhaps glad but wasn't sure she could see the blessing in that yet. A voice told her that dear Father did not have to take care of her financially or otherwise. She could take care of herself. She corrected herself. She could take care of herself.

The lawyer's voice penetrated her reverie. As stipulated by her mother's will, she had to live with her father for a year to get to know him. Upon completion of college, Mr. Moodie would release that money to her.

"No!" she cried as she jumped up from around the table. "No. This is not fair. Isn't her death punishment enough?" By this, she was heaving, trying hard not to cry and break down.

Aunt Carol got up to console her. "Wait, honey. Remember your mother loved you. She would not do anything to deliberately hurt you. You were her world, her everything. Take it easy. Maybe, just maybe some good will come of this."

Maddi wanted to shout and rave. Fate was an evil one. It took the only person who loved her and was now sending her into the annals of the unknown. Auntie C. guided her back to the chair. All this time, Commander Moodie sat motionless. He did not seem perturbed in any way by her reaction.

The attorney cleared his throat again and said it was an emotional decision, but Maddi should give herself time. He encouraged a cooling-off period and that Maddi and the commander should have informal meetings before she went to reside with her father. He expressed empathy for her, but her mother had made him her guardian, so he had the final say. He then excused himself and told them the meeting was over.

As he leaves, Mr. Moodie gets up and addresses Aunt Carol, asking her if he could speak briefly with Maddi alone. Once she leaves, her father addresses her. He explains he was ignorant of her birth until weeks ago. Her mother, Joyce, wanted all three to meet but couldn't have known time wasn't on her side. The day they were to meet was the day she died.

Maddi turns her back. She does not want to hear his platitudes. He can go peddle that somewhere else. She folds her arms. Her father continues that from the sneer on her face to her silence and straight back, he knows she does not believe him. That is unfortunate, as that is the truth. She snorts again. She tells him she does not believe him. However, it is counterproductive going on about it. She cannot supplant herself to the boonies as she has college to attend. He again tries to appease her, telling her for the sake of her mother to let them try. Animosity will make life unpleasant.

Maddi shoots back, asking if responsible adult males shouldn't contact their partners for possible aftermath after intimacies. He inhales, and on a long breath, states he is sorry he did not know he had a daughter. He takes the responsibility of parenting seriously and would never voluntarily walk away. Maddi comes back at him. "Of course not when you could run!"

"Your mom said you were sassy, and that's not a lie. Tread carefully, my daughter."

"Don't call me that!" she spits at him.

"Don't you know," he said conversationally, "that you can't change who your parents are? I will make allowance for your grief. Losing someone you love is never easy."

"Don't do me any favors, Mr. Moodie. Making allowances for my grief—don't patronize me!"

"Okay, Madison Joy, when do we meet? Where is a favorite place for you?" he asked.

Rebellion strong in her back, she tells him nowhere. She tells him she has to get back to school and has no time to indulge in barren pursuits, as she could see no good in that. He changed tactics, asking her to try in the name of Joyce—if not for him, for her mother. He understands she does not trust him, but what of her mother?

She looks at him with hatred. He is gifted with words. He knows that mentioning her mother would undoubtedly be her Achilles' heel. Ablaze with resentment, she tells him she is not available anytime soon. She needs to catch up on assignments, and research papers are due, and, unaccustomed as she is to getting poor grades, needs no distractions.

"Thank you, Mr. Moodie. I am fine," she said.

"For now," he said. "You get your week. The semester ends in five weeks. Here is my card with my number. If you change your mind about meeting between then and now, call me. The number is private. And by the way, your getup didn't fool me. Take care of yourself."

They walk out of the room together but apart. He gives Auntie C. his card with the same request.

Maddi and her aunt leave the law office. They walk in silence as they head for the subway to catch the A train. Maddi can see her aunt's mind churning as she shakes her head several times. As they enter Jay Street station, Maddi notices the platform is not crowded. At least that is something, she thinks miserably.

As the A train pulls into the station, Maddi feels relief and better when she realizes the train is not crowded. They find a corner seat for two. As the doors close, her aunt asks for an explanation, first for the dress. Her aunt gives a smile and then bursts out laughing. She tells Maddi she not only looks ridiculous but crazy. Her aunt continues, "I know you didn't rehearse for this, or you would never leave the house looking like that. Now where did you get that idea?"

Maddi replies, "Well, I did not want to meet the commander. I do not want to live with or get to know him. He has been quiet for seventeen plus years and should let me be. I don't need a father. I have done very well without one. Is he Sir Galahad coming to rescue poor orphan Annie? No, I wish Mom had talked to me before. Yes, immediately after the funeral, Grosman talked to Grandma and Grandpa, and that was how she knew of a father she had labeled deceased. It was just a horror!"

And with that, her eyes brim over. Aunt Carol puts her arms around her and gives her a pack of Kleenex. She dabs at her eyes, unwilling to enhance that frightful look her aunt had indicated. Her aunt starts to talk in a low voice. She tells her that her mother really loved Verne. "She would sparkle when she talked of their romance. He was warm, funny, caring, and was a gentleman. She believed that after another two years of enlistment, he would be ready to settle down. He wanted her to have the opportunity to dance on Broadway, so they had a timeline.

"Somehow, they diverted from that plan. She was reluctant to tell him she was pregnant, but when she finally mustered the courage, he had sailed. She had tried, but no one would give that information. She could not claim family, fiancée, or wife, so that information was not forthcoming. She was horrified at what it would do to his career if she said she was his pregnant girlfriend. She had hoped he would, or their love would lead them back to each other. She waited for two years, then gave up after she was told he died in an accident while removing land mines. Joyce was devastated. She dedicated herself to raising you."

Madison is silent at the end of the narrative. She is tired. She is confused. She is angry at God for taking her mother and resentful that her so-called father failed to search for the girl he'd supposedly love. Now here is this stranger she is to go live with and get to know. To what end, she wonders. She wishes she could block her thoughts. She wishes all the nagging thoughts would just evaporate.

Auntie C. helps her to tidy herself before she gets home. She removes the wig, nose ring, and her aunt produces some Vaseline, which, with tissue, cleans the blue eyeshadow and eyeliner off. She discusses with her aunt the improbable situation she is in. Aunt Carol admonishes her to sleep on things and that God has a plan. She bites back the angry retort and nods. She has to learn to control her temper.

Surprisingly, prior to her mother's death, she never displayed much temper. Now her temper is her banner, open and undisguised. She goes home, gets in bed, and cries.

Chapter 2

Maddi goes back to school and suffers through the condolences of classmates and faculty alike. Many times, the tears threaten, and by some miracle do not fall. Her only witness is the sniffling of her nose. Well, she believes the tears come through her nose. That is better, as allergies are an easier explanation.

She throws herself into her schoolwork with determination and forced gaiety. She cannot wait for the semester to be over yet dreads it. Her life has certainly been like a tumbleweed these last two months and more so since the demise of her mother. She sees the deep dimples in her mother's cheeks and laughing brown eyes, eyes that seemed to sparkle.

Her mother was beautiful, but after the untimely separation from Verne, she had not taken anyone that seriously again. She remembered asking her mother one time if she believed she would ever get married, and she said, "Maybe not."

Maddi would give her all if her mother were back for even one more month. She is afraid of the future. She wishes she had listened more keenly to the lawyer and wished she'd asked Mr. Wonderful about his life now and his family. She knows he is married, and there are children.

Memorial Day looms big and brash. If Memorial Day is May 28, that means in another week college is out, then she is off to the boondocks. She can just imagine what a wonderful time she'll have in Mount Vernon, she among strangers. There have been stilted conversations. She perfects monosyllables. How on earth would she cope a whole year?

A shiver goes through her, a blast of cold air. Suddenly, she is cold on that June day. Her teeth start to chatter. She wraps her arms around her middle to stop the shaking. She is in a state. She cannot go on like this. Now that she does not have tests, term papers, classes, and assignments, her mind takes to wandering, and thoughts of her upcoming trip leave her upset and nervous.

No one shares her trepidation, much less empathizes with her. Her grandparents, Ethel and Benjamin Brookes, are even less so. Maddi believes they never fully got over their last child having a child out of wedlock. They seem not to be aware of her hesitancy and opposition to her father. They had talked with Vernal Moodie. Maddi realized reluctantly she had no support for staying in Brooklyn and defying her mother's request.

Commander V. Moodie came to pick her up June 10. Maddi is packed, equipped with her wig and loud makeup. She resurrects her nose ring. She is ambivalent whether to be a total freak or just a strange person. She puts the wig on, tones down the eye color but outlines her eyes with black liner and adds blue mascara. She surprises herself with conservative lip color in chocolate éclair. The lip gloss belonged to her mother. She thought her mother looked gorgeous in it.

She could not compete with her mother's glamour and grace. She was so beautiful and had no doubt attracted many men. She remembered her mother was dismissive of most men; she never took them seriously. She often said, for some men, women were like chewing gum, always on to the next.

Maddi's lips curl in a smile as she remembers her mother rolling her eyes. She drags a duffel bag and small carry-on to the living room. And there he is—six feet, handsome, trimmed mustache, and manicured hair— her dad!

They set off to Mount Vernon and Westchester County. Her research had made it seem interesting and not the boondocks she had envisioned. There is downtown and several historic landmarks to be explored. In the mood she is in, she has no interest in learning about Mount Vernon. She figures she would not be there long enough to warrant any investment in historical Mount Vernon or otherwise.

She sighs, and the commander looks at her. He inquires if she needs something to drink or eat. She declines any. Clearing his throat, he asks how the semester ended. She is tempted to give a biting remark but refrains at the last minute. In a dull voice, she tells him it ended well. He smiles and asks if she got her usual As. She looks at him with raised eyebrows. She wonders how he knows about her grades and what else he knows about her private life. Determined to say as little as possible, she refrains from asking.

"I know that you have completed a year of college and, like your mom, want to do social work. Social work can be very rewarding, and there are several places for possible employment. There are the court system, counseling juvenile offenders, counseling in schools, the hospitals or nursing homes, and/or rehab. There's a whole world that is open to you. It is commendable for one so young to be focused on studies despite recent incidents that would suggest otherwise."

He looks at her colored hair and nose ring with a half-amused, exasperated look. However, he refrains from any comment. He seems to know that her getup is for his benefit. It is her turn to smile inwardly, hoping her face does not betray her feelings. She glances at him without responding. If he were looking for a talkative traveling company, he had a long wait. She is going against her will to the boonies. She does not feel she has to show gratitude. She feels young and vulnerable and wants her mother. She feels the prick behind her eyes and prays fervently that the tears remain out of view. She wants her dislike to be intact when she reaches his home.

Much rapid blinking and clearing of her throat seem to dissuade the tears. They continue for miles without speaking, and Madison feels good. At last, he gives up trying to make conversation. Just when she gets comfortable, he starts talking again. Maddi rolls her eyes. Why doesn't he give up? She does not want to talk to him. She will when she is ready. She does not want him to dictate when she talks or what topic they talk about. She feels like one of the paper cups floating in Canarsie Pier, bobbing up and down and twirling up and down. Nothing makes sense. She is tired of thinking, of trying to make sense of her mother's untimely death. What, if anything, could she have done? Could the senor have helped if he were in the picture? Why didn't her mother tell her that her father is alive?

Now that school is out, she has all the time to think. She knows what a fertile place one's mind could be for conspiracy theories. She sighs, and her father looks at her. "Don't overthink it. I know you are curious, have questions, but unless you ask, they will just go round and round in your head. There won't be much rest for you. I am very sorry to be meeting under these conditions. I wish there was a way I could make it easier for you. I would very much like to know my firstborn daughter," he ended softly. His softness nearly unravels her composure, and for the first time, she really looks at him. There is sadness in his eyes, pain even, and just for that moment, they connect. She is awash with emotions that possibly they could be father and child. That they share grief and loss of someone they both loved. She breaks the connection and gazes out the window; she does not want to be friends.

Maddi slumps in the seat and, with her head on her left shoulder, closes her eyes. She must have slept because next she realizes, the landscape has changed. She looks around and notices her father watching her. She averts her eyes and rolls her shoulders. She had a crick in her neck and rotated it to get some ease.

"Do you know that you will have to start talking sometime? Think how strange it will be that you are in a household, and you are not talking to your father. Is that what you want? I can only apologize, but I did come to look for your mother and could not find her, and I thought that after three years, she had moved on. Her agent said she had given up and moved away from the city, so I stopped looking. Maybe I should've persisted, but given the age difference, time, her parents, I just thought she forgot about me and moved on. She was so young and beautiful!"

Maddi replies she does not care what anyone thinks. She is not concerned about that. Her father asks her what she wants. She tells him the best solution is to take her back to Brooklyn; that is home, and she belongs there. That seems to annoy him. There is a flash of anger, and she is thrilled at getting a rise out of him. He controls himself with effort. Through clenched teeth, he states it would not happen. She is going to Mount Vernon. She could adopt a mature approach or the juvenile approach and try or not to be reasonable.

The situation is not ideal but, with some give or take, can be amicable. He needs her to be a part of the family.

"You are not suggesting that I call you Daddy, are you? That is laughable and downright preposterous. You are a stranger, someone who clearly abdicated from his responsibility. Ignorance, I hear, is not an excuse!"

"I came back!" he bit out. "We were very—" and he stopped. "I am not explaining anything to you. You need to be civil and respectful, if not for yourself, then for your mother!"

"Leave my mother out of it. You left her. You took your time getting back, so do not behave as if you care because you do not. I was an embarrassment to my grandparents. My mother entered through the back door. She was tainted. She lost her dream. She could tap-dance like Gregory Isaacs, yet very few knew. Yes, she gave it up to be a mother. If you were here, she could have danced in the Forty-Second Street musical. She was that good, but she shelved her dream for me because the father was off fighting a war that had nothing to do with him, and for what? For politicians that are fat with ego, whose children live a privileged existence and do not enlist in the armed forces."

She knew she had gone too far. Ill-advised or not, she knew the soldiers believed in their cause. She is against war and believes that is an area she does not understand and is not interested to know. She does not like war. However, she believes sometimes it was necessary to fight—inevitable, really. She has conflicting feelings; too many innocent people get hurt. She is angry and not interested in being reasonable.

Tears rolled down her cheeks, something she had promised not to do in his presence. She despises the show of weakness. Tears make her vulnerable and immature. Her father pulls off the road to the shoulder. His shoulders sag, and he touches her shoulder. He inhales deeply and tells her they have to talk. There are things that need to be said for both their sakes—must be said. In addition, the past cannot be changed and needs to be faced and come to grips with it. It would be better to accept what cannot be changed and to gently move on. He paused to ask if she would like to step outside. He had parked beneath a sprawling tree that offers shelter from the sun. She gets out not for obedience but because she found the inside confining.

He takes a deep breath and starts to speak. "I met your mother at a time when I was hurt and felt alone. She was young, beautiful, and captivating. She seemed to have a zest for life, for living that was fresh and uncluttered. She had such a joy about her, which was infectious. She was sent to cheer me up. She completely disarmed me with that quick smile and dimples. I was a goner. I loved her, and after my discharge, we started dating.

"She wanted to be a dancer. She loved to dance. We visited Carnegie Hall, Central Park, for picnics and strolls. We read poetry and discussed various topics as well as books, books that ranged from Shakespeare to Great Expectations, Nick Carter, and Ludlum. I am not apologizing for that. As you know, you are the result of our love, and I am not apologizing for that either. My one regret was not knowing about you before now, and whatever you may think, I do love you."

Maddi listened. At times, he seems not to see her or be aware of her presence, as if he were talking to himself. She absorbs what he said about her mother. It is possible that he did love her mother, but how did he not know she existed?

As she tries to clear her mind, he tells her that they should call a truce. He said he has four other children: Daniel, eleven; twins Charles and Chelsea, seven; and Janice, sixteen months. His wife, Phoebe, is a photographer, now only takes photographs of friends and family. Prior to marriage, she worked at Murray's Portraits Studio. He smiles as he asks her if she has any questions, and she shakes her head. He says he just wants the chance to get to know her and vice versa. Also, she has siblings, so she does not have to feel alone as an only child. He asks her to give herself a chance to heal; that spending the summer away from Brooklyn might infuse her with energy and give her a brighter outlook. They are a happy, fun-loving, energetic family. He is sure she will enjoy Mount Vernon.

The request seems reasonable, and Maddi knows that under different circumstances, he would not have to ask, and she knows she would enjoy Mount Vernon. She has never been there.

She is quiet for a long time. He gives her a long questioning look, and she realizes he is waiting on an answer. She nods then tells him yes. He asks if she wants a drink. She looks at him in surprise. He opens a cooler on the back seat and holds a bottle of water, iced tea, apple juice, and cranberry juice.

"Oh!" she said.

"What did you think I was offering?"

Involuntarily, her lips twitched. Is he the corner store? She loves Lipton iced tea. It isn't very sweet and did not taste like tea. The lemon juice in it made the difference. She does not drink hot Lipton, Tetley, or Earl Grey. She drinks herbal tea only. She thanks him for the drink, and they shortly drive on.

He gives her a rundown of Mount Vernon that they'd opted not to be part of the city. When she looks at him, he explains there was a referendum, and Mount Vernon chose not to be part of the five boroughs, so they had their own mayor despite being so close to the Bronx. There is an industrial section, which is to the south. Mount Vernon is divided into north and south. The New Haven Railroad divides the two sections.

There are historical landmarks as well as good shopping. Many of the popular stores are there. In fact, many people traveled there from Connecticut as well as the Bronx to shop there. There is the famous Brush Park over on the south side, so he concluded Mount Vernon is not in the boondocks. Sandwiched between Connecticut and Manhattan was ideal.

He asks if she wants to know more about her siblings. Reluctantly, Madison nods. He tells her Daniel is mischievous and a hopeless prankster. He harasses the twins. Charles and Patrice are typical twins, defending each other. She remarks she thought the twin was Chelsea. He said that was one of her names, said his wife preferred Chelsea, but he liked Patrice and is Chelsea Patrice. She smiles. They are good friends when Daniel is not teasing and defends any one of them even in a fistfight. He believes he has the right to pick on them, tease them, play tricks on them, but no one else has that right. He digs for worms and throws them on the twins. He likes gardening and has a vegetable plot where he grows tomatoes, cucumbers, and peppers. He seems to have a green thumb.

The twins play hide and seek all day if possible. Chelsea Patrice likes to hang upside down from the apple tree and oak tree in the backyard. She is afraid of snails and toads, spiders, and everything that creeps.

Charles's favorite thing is to do cartwheels and stand on his head. He loves karate and is proud to display his muscles. Overall, they are friendly and will make her feel welcome. He ended by saying she should meet them halfway. They are very excited to meet her. His wife is delightful, sweet, understanding, friendly, and kind. With a wry smile, he ends. She is looking forward to meeting her, and they would have girl time.

Madison smiles. It is hard work keeping up this animosity. By nature, she is a nice person, friendly, pleasant, and a joy to know. She is developing into an ace grump. "Okay," she told him, "we have a truce."

His smile is broad, and he seems genuinely happy. After a few minutes, he asks her how long it would take for the dye to leave her hair. She asks why. He looks sheepishly and replies that the color is ghastly. It is designed to scare, and with black lipstick too. Baby Jan will be scared. Madison bursts out laughing. It is the look on his face that had her going.

She asks him how far they are from home, and he said about twenty miles. Madison shakes her head. What would it hurt to be civil for the children's sake? She plans to remove the wig before they reach the house, but she keeps that information to herself. She still did not forgive him for leaving her alone for seventeen years.

They drive in silence, an uneasy truce between them yet at the same time less tense than previously. He asks her conversationally if she has decided how to address him. Maddi jumps. She has forgotten that little issue. She tells him no. He is full of ideas. He suggests Dad, Daddy, or Pops. At her swift intake of breath, she pauses and says softly, or not! She glares at him.

"Think before you speak," came the ominous warning. "Life happens. If I had the power, I would change it so that I held you as a babe and lavished you with the love and affection I gave the other children, but I can't. You don't corner the market on hurt and disappointment. Your mother did the best she could. I wish to God I understood everything, but I don't. You are my daughter, flesh and blood. If I had walked down the street and seen you, I would have known you were my child.

"Look, fighting is debilitating. It's bad for your health. I empathize with your loss. I wish I knew a way to make it go away, but I can't, so please, let's not fight. You are my firstborn, and nothing can change that. You are the product of the love I shared with your mother," he reiterated.

After he finished talking, the pain on his face was undeniable. Maddi felt a pang of guilt but only momentarily. Was there genuine concern for her, or was it for his real family? Was he having second thoughts about their becoming a family and getting to know her? *Well, she thought to herself, let him sweat. Truce or no truce, let him ponder if he had bitten off more than he could chew, per the adage.*

She remembered again the discussion in her Business Law 1 class when they had strayed from the topic and gone into the responsibility of the male after he'd had sexual intercourse with his partner. That is a truth she could not unlearn, and she was not going to try. What about those great soldier stories and love letters being the highlight of their day many times? How could he forget to write? How deep was that love for her mother?

Maddi halted her thoughts. She could not afford Commander Verne to think badly of her mother. In public, she would be civil to him and to her siblings as well as his wife. She felt she had done enough for one day getting under his skin. She mused that at a different time or place, she may not have been so antagonistic.

During his speech, he'd pulled off the road, and now they sat in silence, tense and waiting. She took a shivering breath. She would tell him she would uphold the truce. She took another shaky breath and told him the truce is intact. He gives her a level look and nods with a grim smile. She wished so hard that she could love him freely. She had to trust her mother. She peels the wig from off her head and stuffs it in her oversized shoulder bag. Next, she uses a tissue and wipes the black lipstick off. She uses some Vaseline for good measure, then applies clear lip gloss.

When she is finished, she sees he is watching her. His lips curl in a pleasing smile while shaking his head. "Was that for my benefit?" he asked. "I have often asked myself when children wear that getup how parents handle it. Where had the parents gone wrong? Thank you very much. It means a lot to me."

Maddi permitted a smile then asked him how he handled it. He laughed outright, stating providence intervened, and he did not have to. The car ate up the miles, and they soon reached Fleetwood. He turned into a driveway at the end of the block. Madison got out and stretched, glad she had worn form-fitting cream pants and a navy blue blouse. Her hair braided behind her back, she smoothed her hair, pulled at the pants leg, and looked around.

So this was it. It was a large house from the outside. Her father removed her suitcase from the trunk. Suddenly, she felt a stab of apprehension and looked at her father. He grabbed her hand, gave it a squeeze, and told her it would be fine. Together, they walked to the front door when there clearly was a side entrance.

She did not have a lot of time to ponder the reason because as he inserted his key in the lock, the door flung open. A beautiful woman stood there, beaming. Under different circumstances, Maddi knew they could be friends, but she was in enemy territory. Maddi schooled her features and graciously extended her hands to Phoebe when introduced. However, Phoebe hugged her instead. Maddi was shocked then awkwardly returned the hug. "Oh, come in, Madison, and welcome. It is so nice to meet you. Are you hungry after that long drive? The kids are inside in the dining room."

Maddi follows Phoebe inside. She did not seem to mind that Maddi did not answer. She is surprised at Verne's wife's openness. Her welcome sounded genuine, but time will tell, she decided. They pass through the living room and into the dining room. It is airy and cool. There is a side table and a large eight-seater dining table. The side table has dishes and a platter with crackers, cheese, and fruits—strawberries, grapes, cherries, tangerines, oranges, apples, and watermelon.

Three children seem to magically appear. Phoebe calls them over. She introduces Daniel, the firstborn, and the twins, Charles and Chelsea. The twins look like their mother, while Daniel is a cross between both parents. He has his father's smile, lanky frame, nicely shaped head, and big eyes, and his mother's nose, high cheekbones, and the cleft in his chin. Charles seems a little shy and mumbles hello while the other two give big smiles and high fives. Phoebe decides the dining room is too formal, so they would go to the sprawling kitchen that has a large island with seats.

Maddi asks to use the bathroom so she can wash her hands. Chelsea volunteers to show her. When Maddi and Chelsea return, their father is there, his arm draped across Daniel's shoulders. "Come sit, Madison," he said pleasantly. "Hope there is something here to entice you. However, if there is something you would rather have, let us know."

Maddi assures him she is fine and is very satisfied with what is there. She picks up a plate, puts cheese and fruits on it, and takes some lemonade. Daniel has a big appetite and does not hold back. He seems quite uninhibited. Maddi smiles. Phoebe asks her how the semester was and if she made the dean's list. Maddi tells her she hopes she did, that she had studied, and the results should tell later.

Maddi eats with forced enthusiasm. Another time, another day, she would have enjoyed the fruits, cheese, and lemonade without pretense. She smiles at Chelsea, who smiles back. She turns to her father and asks where the fourth child is.

As if by cue, a baby is heard. Phoebe gets up immediately. "She was sleeping peacefully before you got here. Guess she knows you are home," Phoebe said, rolling her eyes. She got up and playfully pushed Verne on the head. She came back minutes later with a chunky baby girl with bushy hair. Phoebe carries her to Maddi and says, "This is Jan, the fourth member of our quartet."

Maddi touches Jan's hand and smiles at her. "Hello, Jan," she said.

Jan smiles and hides her face in her mother's neck.

"Oh, Jan, you are not shy. This is Madison. Say hello," Phoebe urged.

Jan raises her head, looks at Madison, and smiles. She is a beautiful baby. Maddi is drawn to her. She wiggles from her mother's arms to climb on her father's leg. He picks her up, kissing her cheek. She laughs. She winds chubby arms around her father's neck, chanting, "Daddy."

Her father gives her a piece of cheese, and she eats it seated on his lap. He gives her a sip of his lemonade, and pieces of cheese flow in. He wrinkles his nose. He takes a big sip of his drink. Jan holds on to the glass, and he gives her some more.

Maddi notices the easy camaraderie between the family, and she knows she does not belong here. She smiles grimly to herself. She needs to be by herself. Maddi asks to be excused, and Phoebe gets up and says she will take her to her room. Maddi tells her she hopes she is not inconveniencing the children. Phoebe assures her she is not. She tells her the house has five bedrooms, so there is enough room for her.

Maddi sees her suitcase at the foot of the bed. The bedroom overlooks the back of the house. There is a row of fruit trees. There are apple, pear, peach, and an oak nearby. There is a vegetable plot. She could see squash or pumpkin, callaloo, lettuce, cabbage, beets, and carrots.

Under the oak is a bench. It looks almost white. Maddi figured it is old and weather-beaten, hence the color. The oak offers some shade, and she could imagine sitting there at any time and getting a gentle breeze. There is also an umbrella with chairs. The backyard also has dahlias, rhododendron, hyacinths, and bougainvillea. There is a small patch of manicured lawn in the middle.

Maddi moves away from the window and bounces on the bed. The mattress is firm. She takes another bounce. She knows she should shower but is not in the mood to do so; after all, dirt will only hurt if it falls on you. Furthermore, it was not even four hours since her last bath.

She puts her hands up then slowly flops on her back. She drifts off. As usual, her dream is troubled. She sees her mother lying in the casket with a slight smile. She seems so peaceful, as if sleeping and not dead. She tries to wake her up, but her mother will not budge. "Wake up, Mama, Mom! Please wake up. Wake up! Wake up!"

Maddi comes awake to the sound of knocking on the door and someone asking if she is okay. She struggles up, still foggy from sleep, and croaks yes while clearing her throat. The door opens, and Phoebe steps in. "Are you okay, honey? It sounded as if you were crying out," Phoebe asks, her face concerned.

Maddi assures her she is okay, that perhaps she was dreaming. Phoebe tells her they are going downtown to the open-air market to do some shopping and eat dinner. They would leave in half an hour so they could get some of the fresh produce. They load up in the station wagon and make their way downtown. The vendors are selling everything from produce to arts and crafts.

Maddi has always enjoyed open-air markets. She used to frequent the one at Grand Army Plaza and downtown by the Supreme Court Building. There was a good mixture in the crowd. Vendors were happy hawking their wares. There was good-natured haggling over prices. Phoebe headed for honey, smoked or cured ham, apples, cherries, mangoes, and ripe bananas. The commander carried the shopping bag while Maddi pushed Jan in the stroller. The twins wanted cotton candy, and Daniel wanted Italian ice.

The next stop was at a diner. Luck was with them as a party of eight had just vacated a table, and they sat quickly before the table was properly cleaned. Everyone was tired, so the seats were welcome. Maddi eased one chair out of the way and set up the stroller. Jan did not want to sit anymore and fussed until Maddi took her out, and she sat on her lap.

Soon, a waiter came to wipe the table. Daniel, the twins, and their father went to place the order, stating it would speed up the process. They waited for about fifteen minutes before they were served. Maddi had corn on the cob with grilled chicken, corn tortillas, and water. The twins had chicken and pepperoni pizza. Daniel had a double cheeseburger, large potato wedges, and lemonade. The parents had grilled chicken, baked potato, and iced tea. It was a lively meal. Daniel was willing to help anyone who needed help with his meal. Meanwhile, Jan ate bits of chicken, baked potato, and corn. It was a happy gathering. By the time they were finished, it was close to eight o'clock. As they drove back, Jan fell asleep. They reached home without incident.

Maddi slept fitfully that night. She woke several times in a sweat. She is appalled that the night is so long. She ends up crying herself to sleep about four o'clock. She wakes at six and abandons any attempt at sleeping longer. She turns on her phone and reads her messages. She needed to feel calm. A shower would be desirable, but she did not want to wake the household. She tossed in her mind for a song to soothe her. She could not think of one, so she abandons the idea. It seemed it would be better if she counted sheep.

Eventually, she slept. This time, she dreamt that she saw her mother. She was wearing her white housedress with tiny green and yellow flowers. She was very happy to see her. She screamed in delight and ran toward her mother, arms outstretched. Her mother was smiling, with her hair braided in two and falling on her shoulder. She went to embrace her, and as her arms closed around her mother, she could not feel her. It was as if she held air. The next minute, her mother was gone. She woke with a start. Heart palpitating, she wondered at the strange dream. Why didn't she speak with her? How could she not know how much she missed her?

Maddi rolled over. It is almost eight o'clock, and Maddi makes her way to the bathroom. She would shower and make her way to the kitchen and/or walk in the backyard. She showered quickly, used her moisturizer, and headed back to the room. There are two bathrooms, but she knows the children would use this one. She did not want to inconvenience anyone. The children were affable enough, but she preferred to tread softly. She dressed in shorts and a T-shirt, then used a beret to hold her hair back. She walked quickly and softly to the kitchen, but the commander was there. She was surprised to see him, and her gasp, "Oh, let him know she was there." "Good morning," she said.

"Good morning, Madison. Did you sleep well? I hope everything was satisfactory. I have coffee on."

"No, thank you. I do not like coffee."

"Really! Mmm. Well, what kind of beverage do you like? There is Earl Grey, Tetley, peppermint, and lemon zinger."

"Oh, I am not the hot-beverage person, but when I do, it's herbal tea mostly. I will take the peppermint."

He took a mug and found the peppermint. He turned the kettle on while he stirred his coffee. Maddi noticed that he looked quite domesticated. Well, if she were honest, she did not know anything about CDR Verne Moodie. The kettle boiled and clicked off, and he poured the water for her. She thanked him politely and moved toward the back door. His voice stopped her. "On Saturdays, breakfast is a fun time, and orders are placed. You can order whatever you like, and as chef, I prepare it. So what do you fancy?"

"Nothing, thanks."

"Come on, you must eat. You barely ate yesterday. You can trust my cooking. As you see, we are all robust. So what would you like? I can make a Spanish omelet, cheese or cheese with mushrooms, scrambled eggs, crispy bacon with eggs, or sausage."

"I am sorry. I don't have much of an appetite, but thank you very much. I will just have some fruit. Another place, another time," she said softly, "you would not have to ask me twice. I do not want to take it and then leave it."

He looks at her for a full minute. He seemed about to say something then changed his mind. Maddi felt uncomfortable and made to exit the door when his voice halted her. "You can have your tea here with me. I do not bite," he promised. "We should use this opportunity to get to know one another. We are alone. It is not an ideal situation, but at least I am more than willing to meet you halfway. We agreed to be civil, especially for the younger children's sake, so you need to address me as something."

"You see, Mr. Moodie, you have one up on me. You knew about me, but I did not know about you until—" She stopped as she felt the prick of tears. She inhaled deeply, then began again. "What do you suggest I call you?"

"You can say Dad, Father, or Pop."

"That would imply a relationship, which is a lie. Can I be excused?"

"No. Come here." He grabbed her arm and marched her to the front of the house. He flipped on the light and took her to the entry table, where an ornate big mirror hung. "Look! What do you see?"

Maddi did not know what he wanted her to see. Both their reflections gazed at her. "What?" she asked with a show of temper.

"Your face!"

"What's wrong with it?"

"Nothing, but you are wearing my face. My face! That's what. How can you ever think I would deny you or not acknowledge you? You can substitute heads and never see the difference. You are my daughter. No one can deny that." For the first time, Maddi looked, really looked. She was the spitting image of Verne: smooth forehead, high cheekbones, slightly hollow cheeks, thin upper lip, and full lower lip with a cleft in the chin. She needed help. She looked exactly like him, and the devil drove her. "That must be very inconvenient for you," she spat.

"Careful, my daughter. Tread lightly. One day, you will push me too far."

"What will you do? I am not afraid of you."

"In that case, daughter, you will have a surprise. I do not want to spoil it for you."

Now she had no desire for the tea or anything for that matter. She just wanted to curl up somewhere by herself. She did not want company. However, she walked back to the kitchen, and her father followed close behind. He offered her sugar for her tea, and she declined. She could see he was angry, and she felt remorse. She told him she did not take sugar or any sweetener with her tea. He nodded.

She picked up the fruit and headed outside. She did not want to fight nor bring discord into the household. If someone had asked if she had a temper a year ago, she would have said no. Now the simplest thing set her off. To be honest, it was dear Dad who was the recipient of it in recent weeks. Ever since she knew of him, she had been angry. If she were honest, it stemmed from her mother's illness to her subsequent death. She was mad at the world—everyone and everybody. Her beautiful young mother died and left her alone. She was sure if she had met her father under different circumstances, they would get along, be friends. Maddi could only see a long, bleak future.

Soon, Phoebe came to the kitchen. Maddi did not hear the conversation, but the commander seemed at ease, smiling with his wife. Maddi wondered if he was sharing with her what happened between them. She did not have the nerve to pray because she blamed God for her mother's death.

She blamed the ob-gyn/family doctor as well. Her mother always did pap smears. How could they miss the cancer? It was about two years ago they saw cancer on her cervix. They had used laser treatment to burn the area. She seemed fine, then a year ago, the doctor saw abnormal cells. A routine pap smear showed cancer in the uterus.

After the removal of the uterus, doctors found it had metastasized to the bones, and within a year, she was gone. She often wondered why there are so many medical malpractice suits, but now she understands fully.

She was lost in her thoughts and did not hear or see Phoebe walk toward her. At her greeting, Maddi jumped. Maddi returned the greeting with a smile. Phoebe told her that her father was cooking breakfast and asked what she would like. Maddi thanked her and told her she was not very hungry and preferred to have a bowl of fruit. Maddi assured her that the fruits were adequate.

Sometime later, the rest of the children rushed into the kitchen. It was loud and jolly. Maddi could hear the laughter. Daniel stuck his head out and called to her. She waved and uttered a cheery greeting. Chelsea followed suit with a greeting while Charles simply waved. Maddi ate her fruits and was content. She could see the closeness of the family members. She knew she was an outsider. Well, she did not plan to hang around, so it was okay to keep her distance. She did not want to bond with the children. She could see them in the kitchen. Daniel walked outside and asked her about breakfast. She replied patiently that she did not want breakfast. He told her that he ordered an omelet with the works. Maddi smiled and asked what the works were. With exaggerated patience, he told her, "mushroom, bell peppers, cheese, and ham." Maddi laughed. "How do you manage to eat so much, and it does not show?" she laughed.

He just laughed. He was eating an apple with enjoyment. He looked at her, and his head tilted. "You are thin. You need some meat on these bones," he said cheekily, touching her hands. "No meat," he said, shaking his head and enjoying himself.

She made a fist at him playfully, and he jumped back. He set off to see if the cook had his order ready. Maddi watched him go and knew there would be more challenging times ahead. The children were all likable. Maddi smelled trouble. Maddi stayed outside and nursed her fruit bowl.

About half an hour after she left the kitchen, she saw Phoebe enter with Jan. Before long, Jan was holding her cup with milk. Maddi closed her eyes and thought of her grandparents in Brooklyn, then idly wondered if her father's parents were alive, and if so, did he tell them of his indiscretion?

She smiled without humor. She would have loved to hear that conversation. She wondered how old they were and what they looked like. Whom did the great Verne look like? What did it matter anyway? She would find out soon enough. It was enough being with this nuclear family and she the plus-one.

She admits she has the right to be sad but has to fight deep depression. She closes her eyes and prays because she feels helpless and out of choices. She must help herself. She can call Pam, Joan, or Phil. She debates whom to call first and chooses Janet. She will place the call about ten o'clock. That will give her a window to think of something else.

She relaxes on the bench, glad of the opportunity to slow her churning thoughts. She will think happy thoughts. She is sure to make the dean's list again. That is something to be proud of. One thing she is good at is test-taking, so there is no fear of not doing very well.

Chapter 4

She began to hum the song "Sing the Clouds Away." She hummed all three verses. As she finished the chorus, she did feel better. She sang it repeatedly until she forgot about sadness or depression. To her, depression is a graveyard. Once ventured in, it was a maze to get out of. She must take care of herself if she wants her father to accept she can take care of herself.

With her thoughts less chaotic, she got up and walked to the kitchen. When she entered, Jan began to fuss. Maddi walked over to her, and she stretched her hand to Maddi. She just wanted to shake her hand, but Jan let go of her father's neck, reaching for Maddi. Maddi took her. Phoebe broke in laughter. "Well, I do not believe it! No kidding. I am surprised. Never thought I'd ever see the day the king gets dethroned. Now I feel so much better."

Maddi did not know what Phoebe was talking about. Her blank look gave her away. Phoebe explained that Verne is Jan's favorite, that once present, she abandons you, but it is the first time she left him voluntarily for someone else. She is happy at the turn of events. Maddi finally got it. She smiles. That tasted like victory to her.

She walks away with Jan in her arms. Maddi was sure she heard Verne say under his breath, "Traitor," to the smiling Jan.

Maddi walks with Jan back to the bench. Jan sits on her lap. She puts her cup down, then stands on Maddi's thighs. She bounced up and down. Maddi decides to teach her name. She tells Jan, "Maddi," while pointing to herself. Jan obediently repeats it, making a chorus of it.

After breakfast, she offers to wash the dishes. Phoebe declines, stating that it is Daniel's chore. Daniel protested that if Madison wants to do the dishes, then he has no objection. Everyone laughs at his speech. As a compromise, Maddi helps.

The next day, being Sunday, they all went to church, except Maddi. She asked to be excused. She was not up to scrutiny up close or otherwise, and worst, did not want to answer the same question repeatedly. She did not want to exchange polite conversation with strangers. She would watch Daystar and listen to Joel Osteen or T. D. Jakes or Crystal Cathedral. Maddi calculated she would be alone for about two hours.

After the family left, Maddi turned on the television. She found the station and watched Joel. He was an interesting speaker. Some people welcomed his unorthodox approach to preaching. Many people loved him, but some thought he was more of a motivational speaker. Maddi did not care. She liked Joel. He was a storyteller, and she liked that. He did not preach fire, brimstone, hell, and damnation. There are enough preachers who thrive on damnation and hell. If he motivates people to do better, be better, to love and forgive, then where is the harm in that?

Maddi reckoned she needed Joel's optimism and encouragement to see a loving and caring God. She was angry at God for taking her mother, so she needed forgiveness. Joel did not disappoint; he talked about forgiveness. Well, T. D. Jakes said, "Let it go." Maddi mused that was easier said than done. By then, the family was back.

Maddi assisted Phoebe with dinner preparations. She was making tuna Florentine, mac and cheese, and oven-fried chicken. Everything was prepared, ready to put in the oven about four o'clock for six o'clock dinner. That left about three hours of downtime. Jan fell asleep in her father's arms and was placed in her playpen in the den. Phoebe reminded the children about summer camp and to find their clothes and whatever else they would need. They went out, and Maddi picked up an O, The Oprah Magazine. Oprah stared back at her, and she leafed through to find an interesting article. She read an article on money management. Not much of it stuck. However, she hoped it would come back to mind when needed. She curled up in the chair and went to sleep. She came awake feeling as if something were crawling on her. To her surprise, Daniel was pulling a piece of thread across her face. She made a fist, and he jumped back. She figured that's what twelve-year-old boys do. She helped Phoebe with the dinner and made a fresh salad.

The next day, the older children went to camp, and this routine continued. She became more and more attached to Jan. The two got along very well. Phoebe got her camera out, taking pictures of birds and butterflies and occasional shots of family members.

Jan was ridiculously photogenic. She did not know how to take a bad picture. With one quick take, Phoebe took her picture while she played with Jan. Phoebe was incredibly talented, and it showed. Phoebe told her one day how much she looked like her father, that she, Jan, and Verne were identical. She laughed that she has never seen anyone look so much alike. Maddi smiled without responding. However, it became a source of amusement for Phoebe. One day, while holding Jan, Verne walked up, and she snapped him. The picture was unbelievable. Maddi was startled at the resemblance. From then on, Phoebe would smile each time she looked at Maddi.

They settled into a routine. She played with Jan, took her outside in her stroller for short walks, or they stayed in the backyard if it was not too hot. She and her father were polite housemates. She was polite, especially in front of the children. Several times, Phoebe tried to engage her in conversation about her father, but she did not want to talk. What would she say to her? Your wonderful husband left me for seventeen years and never looked back. She was still hurting that he knew nothing about her. Isn't it widely held that the heart would know if you were truly in love with someone? Did the mortar from the war stop his ears?

Her father did not fare any better with her. She always answered in monosyllables to discourage conversation. She was not unhappy, as Jan was lovable and a delight and made up for the rift between her and Dad. She was careful around the family to be polite and pleasant. She noticed at times that Daniel eyed her with curiosity, but she ignored him.

It was the second week of camp, and Maddi had her routine: shower, breakfast, bathe Jan, and take her for a walk. Her father decided he would join her. Phoebe came out, heard Verne's words, and told them to wait. She got her camera and took quick snaps of them. Maddi smiled but was inwardly irritated. She must watch out for Phoebe. She seemed determined to photograph her with the father. She was not taking ownership of Verne Moodie. She realized she cannot stop him as Jan is his daughter and did not want Phoebe asking questions.

They set out at a leisurely pace while Jan laughed and pointed at anything and everything. Verne asked how she is settling in and what, if anything, she needed. She assured him she is fine and needs nothing. She added for good measure, "My life is amazing. I meet four siblings, a stepmother, and a father after seventeen years. What can I possibly want? A man who was so in love with my mother but never bothered to keep in touch with her never came back. Yes, my life is great."

By the look in his eyes, she knew her barb hit home. She felt pleased with herself. He had held her wrist, and he said softly, lips barely moving, "You are very wrong. I wrote your mother, and later, I came looking for her, but I did not find her. Even a fool would know you are my child. Why would I not accept you? I wish I had known, and I cannot change the past. If I could, I would, but it is out of my hands. We can be a family. Give yourself a chance to get to know me."

"A delightful story. How is it I am just hearing it, and where did you go to look, Prospect Park? You cannot believe my mother would be there, do you? Or perhaps it was Central Park."

"No, Madison, I visited your grandparents' house, left my number for your mom, and later sent her letters at that address."

"My grandparents never mentioned you visited there."

"How would you know, seeing that you did not know me?"

"Grandma and Grandpa would have told Mother. My mother would tell me. What I heard in the lawyer's office did not mention any such contact, and that letter from her did not mention that either. Can we not talk anymore?"

"I have no reason to lie, Madison. I am not one of your little friends afraid of reprisals. Shirking my responsibility is outside my range of expertise."

Maddi gave a snort and a disbelieving look. He seemed about to say something but changed his mind. Jan was looking at them and pointing. Poor Jan; she was forgotten while they argued. Well, Maddi smiled and started to run, and Jan started to laugh. Maddi sat in her favorite seat and put Jan to the right of her. He picked Jan up and bounced her on his knees. Jan laughed and screamed. He kissed her, much to her delight, and she shouted, "Daddy!"

Verne was pleased. Madison wondered if that was to make her jealous. She reasoned she was his child, although he intruded on their morning outing. He asked if she were ready, and she got up. He put Jan back in the stroller.

Jan became sleepy on the way back and was asleep by the time they reached home. Verne took her to her room. Maddi walked to the kitchen for water. She took her water bottle from the fridge. She would stay inside and cool off before going in the backyard. She went to her room and picked up her crossword puzzle book. She flopped in the overstuffed chair in the den.

She jumped when she heard her name. She looked around and saw the book on the floor. She knew she fell asleep. The next minute, Phoebe was asking if she wanted to go shopping with her. Maddi asked about Jan and was told her father could have daughter-dad bonding. If she stayed, she would be with Verne, and he may want to continue the earlier conversation, and if she goes shopping, then Phoebe may want to discuss her relationship with her father. She had to decide which was more palatable. It may seem strange if she refused shopping. Normal young girls loved shopping. She argued she was not a normal young girl but accepted Phoebe's invitation.

They drove downtown and parked near the church. Maddi loved the row of trees on the block. It provided shelter from the sun and a slight breeze ruffled the leaves. Phoebe visited Wright's Portraits, dropped off three rolls of film, and bought half a dozen. From the greeting of the owner, Phoebe was a friend and customer. Phoebe introduced Maddi, and she nodded politely with a smile at Jonas Wright. He asked how she liked the town, and she told him she liked it, though different from Brooklyn but in an amazingly comfortable way.

Phoebe walked into a children's store. She wanted rompers for Jan. Phoebe bought four, and they were soon on the way to Macy's. Phoebe told Maddi she used to be a size nine but, four children later, was bordering on a thirteen. Maddi eyed her and leaned her head, considering she had hips, not fat.

Phoebe chatted while they browsed the racks. She told Maddi her favorites were the marked-down ones. They searched, and Phoebe found two Gloria Vanderbilt dresses. "These may not be shoes, but even if I have to pare my body like Cinderella's sisters, I am buying them and wearing them," declared Phoebe.

Maddi burst out laughing. She could not contain her laughter. Two elderly ladies looked at them curiously, but by then, Phoebe was laughing too. Phoebe tucked them possessively under her left arm. They continued to search. She looked at a lilac dress by Gloria Vanderbilt, and Phoebe urged her to buy it. It was a size six. They carried six dresses and fit them. One was snug, almost tight, but Phoebe said she would lose weight, so the six dresses, four for Phoebe and two for Maddi, totaled $102. Phoebe was happy. She said she shopped before for the children and Verne.

They bought Italian ice as they headed for the car. It was hot, but going in and out of the stores was not oppressive, plus with people going in and out of the stores, you got a whiff of cool air. Before long, they reached the car. They ate their ices while the car cooled. After they finished, Phoebe turned to Maddi. "I really enjoyed being with you today. It was fun. I loved hearing you laugh. Your face lights up! You should laugh more often!"

"Thank you, Phoebe, but you are very funny. Cinderella's sisters?" said Maddi with a smile.

Phoebe looked at her with a grin.

"I know what you are thinking and what you are going to say, but don't," she told Phoebe.

Phoebe looked innocently at Maddi, lifted her shoulders, and pulled her fingers across her lips. She was unrepentant. She smiled with contentment, and then she said conversationally, "You know, that's why Jan relates so well to you. She knows who you are. Even she knows, and is it so bad? Is there not a common ground, honey? He loves you, you know. He cannot help himself. If he did not, he would have to hate himself and Jan as well. No one has ever challenged Verne for Jan's affection except you, and you did not even try."

"Phoebe, I know you mean well, but it is complicated. You would not understand," said Maddi.

"But honey, you are here with us. The stilted conversation and long silence cannot be good for you. I wish there was something I could do for you. You are a beautiful young lady, but who still needs her parents. We are concerned for you. We want to help you."

"Thank you, Phoebe, but I am fine. There is nothing that I need now. I see you are a genuinely nice person, and I can see where Jan got her personality from, but I am the child of your husband thrust upon you. Why should you care whether I am happy or fit in? I am not your responsibility or anyone else's at this point. In a couple of months, I will be eighteen years old, and I will go back to Brooklyn."

"Look, darling, how could I not care about you? What kind of person would that make me? Yes, you are Verne's child, and thank God. But you and your mom were way before my time. I know it could not have been easy, but she raised you single-handedly. And what a young lady you are, the friction notwithstanding. I can only hope mine turn out to be like you."

Maddi searched her face and could detect no deceit. Phoebe touched her face as tears trembled on her lids. She hugged her so hard, Maddi could hardly breathe. Phoebe smiled. "Thank you for what you said about my mom. I really appreciate it. Few people get it."

"I do, darling. One time, when Charles and Chelsea were about twenty months, Verne came home and found all of us crying. Poor man! Did not know what to do: comfort the children or his wife. I dozed off on the sofa, and they climbed out of their playpen. They emptied their bags I usually kept packed, then I had left a pack of wet wipes, baby oil, and baby powder, and they went to war.

"When I saw the trail through to the kitchen and living room, I just cried. My crying upset them, although I do not know what they had to cry about. They made the mess. I had to clean it up. Oh, and yes, the dinner burned, and the smoke detector went off. Guess I just felt sorry for myself," Phoebe ended with a laugh.

Maddi laughed. She could not help herself. She tried to imagine Commander Verne taking charge of the situation. Much different from commanding soldiers! Maddi wondered aloud what they had for dinner. "Oh, nothing much. Just Chinese," and she laughed in delight. "I was sure I was finished with childbearing, but we had decided prior to have four children, so we talked about it and decided we would wait. I have no regrets even if Jan is a daddy's girl. At least she was until recently."

Phoebe gave Maddi a cheeky look. Maddi smiled and refused to take the bait. She liked Jan. She really is a sweetheart. She has her mother's personality. That explains why she is so good-natured and loving.

"Madison, Verne would not deliberately walk away. So far, I know your mother was quite lovely. He used to nurse a picture of her when I first met him. He was not interested in me, and after seeing a picture of your mom, I understood why. We only started dating about three years after his return. I believe he had given up on your mother by then. I hesitated before having one date with him because of that picture he had. I did not want to be caught on the rebound. I did not take his interest in me seriously. I preferred to hone my craft of photography. I was working at Wright's, and although I was good, I needed to be better. It was about four years after his return from the war that we dated seriously. Well, the end results speak for themselves."

Maddi felt obligated to respond, which she did slowly. "I know, Phoebe. I just cannot help how I feel."

"Just think about it. We are a family. You are the firstborn, the older sister of Daniel, Chelsea, and Charles. Jan loves you. You cannot deny that. And forgive Verne. Give him the benefit of the doubt. The fact that your mom loved him should count for something. They talked. She must have forgiven him, and she wanted you two to be united. You have nothing to lose and everything to gain."

Maddi considered Phoebe's words. What did she really have to lose? She was angry. She had gotten used to being the daughter of a dead soldier. It hurt to know he was alive and, well, with a family. How many times did she want a father? She imagined he was handsome, loving, and kind. It was disappointing that he was MIA or dead.

Maybe she should rejoice because he was alive, but she was resentful. She did not begrudge his life because she liked his kids. If her mother were alive, it would be different. She would serve as a buffer between them, and the unification would be easier, but she could not stem the resentment. Normally, she is fair, open-minded, and a pacifist, but to know he was living in New York and she never met him rankled. He was close, and he did not know about her. She wondered if Verne had come back, would her mother have four additional children.

Maddi sighed. She could see the questions in Daniel's eyes. She wondered how long politeness would keep him silent. What a mess! She decided to put all this from her mind and remember the two beautiful dresses and where she could wear them. "I will try my best to close the divide between my father and me. Growing up without a father was difficult. There were many a day I yearned for a father. My mother taught me to ride a bike, to shoot hoops, and play rounders. She worked long hours sometimes, and despite that, managed to be at most of my games in addition to dance rehearsals and recitals. She was so energetic," Maddi ended.

Chapter 5

Phoebe decided to buy dinner. She went to a West Indian restaurant and bought roti with curry chicken, jerk chicken with rice and peas, escovitch whiting with fries, macaroni cheese, barbecue chicken, and carrot juice. Maddi loved roti, and it was tantalizing her nose. That put her in a good mood.

When they headed home, Phoebe turned the radio on Lite FM. The voice of Journey filled the car: "Open Arms." Maddi closed her eyes and shook her head. It was one of her mother's favorites. The haunting, poignant music filled the car. Phoebe sang loudly after declaring how much she loved it. A series of other love songs deemed pleasant listening followed. They rode in comfortable silence, humming snatches of verses and choruses as known.

Verne met them at the door. He inquired if there was anything left in the stores. Phoebe laughed, kissing his cheek. Maddi saw him smile in turn. She noticed again the easy camaraderie between them. He said he could smell curry and jerk chicken. Moments later, the children came from camp. They were sent to wash and come back for dinner. Meanwhile, Maddi washed her hands in the powder room. As usual, the evening meal was loud and boisterous. Jan woke up, so the whole family had dinner together. Jan was a little subdued, but that was because she was not fully awake.

A lively game of Scrabble ensued alongside draft. Verne and Daniel played draft. You could hear Daniel loud and laughing. "Take that and take that"—pumping his fist. They played for a long time. Maddi egged the others on. She helped Chelsea with her word formation, which took her from last place to first place. She was delighted and hugged Maddi. Chelsea was more friendly and more comfortable around Maddi.

It was then their father cleared his throat and told them he had an announcement. "Oh, boy! What now, Dad?" Daniel blurted out.

"Well, I got a call from Jen that she and William are stopping by tomorrow for a brief visit on their way to New Jersey."

"Are you gonna let her, Dad?" Chelsea wailed.

"Can I stop her? That woman is like a hurricane, blows in high velocity, and any small craft not tied down gets tossed on the sea; then I get to clean up. You just must remember, though, half the things she says are not meant to be malicious. She just talks without thinking."

"So, Verne, how is it you are just telling us?" asked Phoebe.

"Well, Phoebe, for a number of reasons. I did not want to spoil your appetite. I wanted my share of dinner just in case you decided to punish me for the news, and I wanted you all with full bellies before I gave the news. I felt it would go over better, and see, it does," he ended with a smile.

"Verne, you coward," Phoebe said with a laugh and threw a cushion at him.

He caught it deftly and said, "Self-preservation, my dear Watson, self-preservation. Come, Madison, take a look at our night sky. You can see actual stars." She made to put Jan down, but she wrapped her arms tightly around Madison, shaking her head. "Oh, you can take your tail with you," he said, kissing Jan's cheek. He opened the door, and they went to the backyard. She obediently looked for the stars and saw them. The sky was dark but not inky. There was a calm there, even peaceful. Maddi realized the request involved more than star gazing. "What is this about?" Madison asked after about five minutes. She was sure he must know she was not stupid enough to believe it was about stars.

"I have been remiss in telling you about my folks. I wanted you situated first as they can be a handful. It is not everyone. They are personable once you get to know them, but my sister Jennifer is a different matter. She is outrageous. She says the darndest things, a mouth without a filter. She has always been like that, so you will need to know that, or you will be offended."

"Is that the only sibling?" Madison asked, a little intrigued.

"No, there is James, who lives in New Jersey and is divorced with one son, James Allan Jr. And there is Amina, quite the opposite of Jennifer, married to a doctor and has three children. She lives in Connecticut too. I did not want to overwhelm you with my siblings and their oversized personalities when you just came, but it is necessary to tell you about them."

"Why, you sound as if you care," she said.

"I did not come outside to fight. When you get to know me, you will see I protect my own. I just want to prepare you for Jen. She talks too much at times. My parents, Harold Vernon Moodie and Edith, live in Florida part-time. They are called snowbirds. Once it gets cold, they fly down, and once the snow is over, they come back. They have been doing that for about seven years now. You will like them.

"Jan is easily their favorite, but we will see this time around. They are on a European cruise now and will go back to Florida before venturing home. You will be okay. If Jen gets out of hand, I will handle her. You just cannot be timid around her. Do you have any questions?"

"Do your parents know about me? Oh, that is a silly question. Of course they do. That is part of the reason Jennifer is coming, right? Coming to see Verne's illegitimate child!"

"For heaven's sake! You are twisting things. The thought never crossed my mind. You are mine. I dare the person to pin that label on you," he growled. "You are my daughter. End of story!" His handsome face looked grotesque in the half-light. Maddi shivered. He was fierce when angry, and for the first time, she thought maybe there was regret for not knowing about her. Maybe he feels guilty if he is the type thought to be always in control and in charge. "Okay, I am sorry," Maddi said softly. "I do not want to fight either. What time will Jennifer be here?"

"Anywhere after ten-thirty or so. I will be grilling, so I will set that up before the descent. Breakfast will be the usual affair, nine-ten. The weather should be fine in the eighties and maybe a gentle breeze. What could be better?"

"True. What could be better? Did you fight with Jennifer growing up?"

"All the time. She was mischievous and antagonizing. She always got me in trouble because I had to defend her from children who wanted to beat her up. She provoked everyone. There was this time she called this boy cheesecake on her way home from school. We heard he liked this girl, bought her a slice of cheesecake, hid it in his locker at school, and it was three days later before he got up the nerve to give it to her. It was stale by then, of course.

"No one knew how the story got out, but he was called cheesecake behind his back. Oh, no, my sister could not do like others. She called him to his face! He was built like an ox and was going to fight her, so I jumped in. I got one good jab off, and he punched me in the gut. I saw stars.

"After a minute or two, still doubled over, I ran into him headfirst and knocked him off his balance. I did not wait around. I ran home. Jennifer followed minutes later, as cool as a cucumber, telling me what a good job I did. I promised her that was the last fight I would get in because of her."

Maddi smiled. "I guess she was not sorry."

"You guessed it. I was happy when I graduated. Keeping Jennifer safe was a full-time job."

Maddi smiled. She could not believe he could be intimidated by anyone, but apparently, he was. There is a lot of information to process. This is enough, she thought. Tomorrow, she would meet the family hurricane. Maddi smiled. Bring it, Jennifer. I am here waiting, but not as a sitting duck. Her mom used to say forewarned is forearmed. She would not be broadsided, plus she has nothing to prove. She is not concerned about people's opinions of her.

Decision made, she turned back to her father, smiled, and said good night, then she thanked him for telling her about his family. He nodded but said there is another issue that needs attention.

"What is that?" Maddi asked.

"Me—how to address me."

Maddi looked askance. "Oh!" she said as light dawned. "Yes. What do you prefer, Dad, Father, Daddy?"

"How about Pops?"

"No. What of Sire?" she finished unrepentantly.

"You are a real Moodie, you know. Otherwise, you would not have this gall. I see you read your share of fairy tales."

Maddi smiled but did not apologize. In truth, none of the titles appealed to her, but she conceded she had to call him something. She tried the titles in her head, then finally said Dad. She bade him a hasty good night and headed indoors.

Saturday dawned bright and clear. There was more activity this Saturday than the last. Daniel said he was excited as he always had time for a barbecue. He got the igloo out and the coal for the grill. Shortly after, he left with Verne to buy ice, hamburgers, buns, extra sodas, juice, plates, cups, napkins, chicken legs, ketchup, and barbecue sauce. In the meantime, Phoebe took chicken legs and proceeded to half-cook them to hasten the time on the grill. She also put the coal in the grill to await her husband's return.

It was ten-thirty, and Jennifer was not there yet. Maddi dressed in jean shorts and a pretty light top crossed in the back. Phoebe wore khaki capris with a T-shirt. Jan was in floral rompers, while the twins wore cutoff jeans and T-shirts. Additional chairs were placed under the tree along with a quilt blanket. Maddi eyed it, thinking how suitable it was for her and Jan.

Shortly, Verne and Daniel returned with their purchases. Maddi helped pack the ice and added the juice, water, soda, and beer. She helped with the corn, stripping away the extra leaves. Verne got the fire started. Maddi guessed that was not a challenge for a soldier. Soon, roasted corn was wafting on the breeze. This was the reason Maddi loved summer; the smell of a charcoal grill never failed to tantalize her nose. She loved the scent.

Before the first corn was roasted, Jennifer and Will came. She arrived like thunder, loud and boisterous. Jan ran toward Maddi as she hugged her brother. Will, much quieter, followed, slapping Verne on the back. Jennifer shouted to the kids, and they chorused, "HI, Auntie Jen!"

Verne waved to Maddi, and she walked over, and he introduced them. Jennifer's eyes looked like saucers, and Maddi laughed. "Oh my God, Verne. She is the spitting image of you. This is no maybe! This is sure Verne's baby! Honey, let me look at you," Jennifer said while turning Maddi around. "Damn it, Verne, she even has the birthmark on her shoulder!" and she burst out laughing.

Maddi smiled. Jennifer is outrageous. She has no filter. Her husband, Will, said, "Jen!" shaking his head. "Will," he said, shaking her hand. "Forgive my wife. It is nice to meet you, and condolences," he ended softly.

Maddi liked the tall, slim man with salt-and-pepper hair. He turned toward Jan, who was squirming and trying to get out of Jennifer's arms. She willingly let Will take her, whirling her around. She laughed. "Why so formal? She is family, ain't she? Sorry, honey, I know about your mother.

Such a pity and so young too. You know, I saw your mom once while she was out with Verne. She seemed shy, but I guess she wasn't really very shy," Jennifer said.

Maddi's eyes narrowed. She knew what Jennifer was implying. Before she could respond, her father said, "For Christ's sake, Jennifer! You are worse than a bull in a china shop. Just stop now. It's supposed to be a fun, pleasant day with family."

Madison thanked him with her eyes. Jennifer didn't know how close she came to Maddi's telling her where to go and how to get there. She should never believe she cornered the market on being tactless or outspoken. Maddi smiled grimly. She was sure Jennifer would do it again. She awaited the opportunity to set her straight.

After the awkwardness, everyone got corn. Jan eagerly shared Madison's. Soon, Verne donned an apron and cap. The apron clearly said, "Do not kiss the cook." He put hot dogs, beef, and chicken, as well as hamburgers and turkey burgers, on the grill. The smell of grilled meat teased Madison's nose. She just loved the smell of roasting meat. Madison got a turkey burger for herself and her friend Jan. They sat under the tree on the quilt.

As they sat, Jan abandoned her plate for Madison's. Maddi laughed. She took a sip of Madison's drink, and pieces of turkey floated freely in the water. Thank you, Jan, Madison thought, drinking from the same cup.

Jan then started to blow bubbles in the water while encouraging Madison to drink it. Madison whispered to her to give it to her mother. Jan ran with it to her father instead, encouraging him to drink. He wrinkled his nose when he saw the goodies in it. He pointed her back toward Madison. "Oh, no! There is your buddy. She likes it. See, baby?"

Jan turned and ran toward Maddi. By this time, everyone's attention was on the three of them. "Oh, all right. Jan, make sure you do not speak, laugh, or play with anyone except me, okay? Only me!"

Jan nodded, as if understanding Maddi's directions. At that, everyone laughed. Verne kissed her. After that, the day passed pleasantly enough. There was a rowdy game of touch football with the four men while the ladies played Scrabble. As the shout for the last round of food came, all games ceased. Replete, everyone was sitting and talking while music came from two speakers outside the back door. The sound of Kenny G.'s "Songbird" was hauntingly familiar, and Madison closed her eyes. Her mother loved Kenny G. There was the familiar prick of tears. Gathering Jan in her arms, she clasped her close to her chest till the feeling waned.

As the sun was going down, so was Jan's head on her chest, so Madison picked her up and headed indoors. She waved Phoebe away, telling her she would put Jan to bed. "Poor baby! You are tired. You did not sleep today, not for a minute, so you will sleep all night. Jan, you are the best baby, next to me, of course," she ended with a laugh, kissing her cheeks. Maddi got a washcloth and basin to give Jan a sponge bath. The adage "dirt don't harm except it falls on you" came to Maddi's mind, and she smiled.

As she left the room, she encountered Jennifer. She smiled and made to go by, but Jennifer stopped her. "Madison, or is it Maddi?"

As Maddi shrugged, she continued, "I am sorry about you losing your mom. I did meet her once with Verne, you know. So you lived in Brooklyn all this time. Guess she had to work very hard to take care of a child by herself. She was rather young, wasn't she?"

"Thank you, Ms. Jennifer. We were fine, but just so you know, my mother is not up for discussion now or in the future. Just saying," she adds just for sass.

"Darling girl, why so prickly? I just want to offer my condolences and just commiserate," said Jennifer.

"Okay, where are your children? It is summer, and school is out. How is it they are not here today?" asked Maddi sweetly.

"Why?" she asked.

"I believe this is the perfect time for a family outing, so we can commiserate at the same time."

"Look, missy, I do not know what you are driving at," said Jennifer.

"Well, my father told me you have two children and thought they would be here with you. I figured they may be closer to my age is all," said Maddi innocently, looking wide-eyed.

"I don't get you. I'm not sure if you are sassing me or not. One is doing summer school and did not want to make the trek home after in the traffic, and the other is doing an internship at a law firm. Is that okay with you?"

"Now who is being prickly? Are they not teenagers? Here I am, a stranger to a whole bunch of persons I never heard about until now. I get a brief outline of my dad's siblings, and it's unusual to ask about the cousins. They are college students, are they not? Maybe I am waiting to talk college with them. But it is okay, Ms. Jennifer. Don't need to talk at all. Let me see if the others need help outside. Jan is already fast asleep."

"The baby seems to like you. Last time I checked, she was a daddy's girl. As an only child, you seem very comfortable dealing with Jan," said Jennifer.

"I have a lot of practice," Madison replied.

"Oh, church and babysitting. There is a nursery at church for babies twelve months old to three years old. I like babies and children in that order," said Madison.

"What are you studying? You are at NYU, aren't you?"

"Yes, NYU, and I am enrolled in social work, and yes, my mother is the inspiration," Madison said, her grim tone not lost on her aunt. I do not care what she thinks of me.

"Look, Madison, I am really sorry about the loss of your mom. Losing your mom at any age is rough. I wish we were there, and you knew about us. I wonder why your mom never tried to find us, you know—Verne's family. That is so strange. Why would any woman voluntarily have a child by herself? Hmm. Didn't she know Verne's last name?" she finished. The look on her face tells the story she said aloud. She put her hand to her mouth and moved toward Madison.

Madison backed away from her in horror. "Ms. Jennifer, you do not have a monopoly on a big mouth nor on being ignorant and obnoxious! You started outside, and I let it go, but now that we are talking assumptions, it's my turn. Two children only, but because of who their mother is, they stay away. Secondly, it is said soldiers are heroes, but they err. Your husband is the hero. Look who he is married to. And thirdly, all that gray hair he acquired is a part of his largesse. What, you lasso him? Why is he still married to you?" Madison ended.

Her breathing was shallow, and her chest was heaving, squaring off with Jennifer. Miraculously, Verne entered the hallway. The flash of Madison's eyes and heaving chest painted a picture for him. "What in tarnation is going on?" he asked. "Madison." He held her and pulled her into his arms.

She was trembling and breathing hard.

"I swear, Jennifer, if you hurt my child, I will take you apart."

Instinctively, Madison burrows in the comforting arms.

"No need to worry, brother of mine. She is no Chihuahua but a German shepherd. You do not have to fight for this one. Another time, Madison, we will resolve our differences. We are family. We must never fight. I cannot wait for Mom and Dad to meet you. It will be interesting," she said with a smile that never reached her eyes.

"And so will I. So will I. I thought the Gulf War was my last battle, but so be it. I have not lost my edge," he said too softly.

Her father's arm felt like steel the longer she stayed. "Dad, I can't breathe," said Madison.

He seemed not to hear.

"Dad, I can't breathe," she said again.

His face showed surprise as he looked at her. "Oh! Oh!" And he lets her go. He gives her a long look. "Are you okay?"

"My Achilles' heel is my mother. Anyone who crosses that line, it is on, no-holds-barred," she said on a shuddering breath.

"Well, you do not look worse for wear. I guess you thwarted Jennifer this time, but she can be a real pal when she is ready. Once she knows you are not a pushover, she will cool it. Just know that every so often, she will go haywire, and the tart tongue will sweeten," he said with a slight smile. "What does she mean you are a German shepherd?"

"Are you sure you want to know? No. I think perhaps you are better off not knowing." Shaking her head, she smiles and goes through the back door.

With music playing, they start to clean up. After cleaning, the children get the Scrabble. To make it interesting, Madison decides to join them. She teams up with Chelsea in a boys-versus-girls game.

After about an hour or so, Jennifer and Will say their goodbyes. Everything seems civil and above scrutiny. Madison smiles as she turns and walks to her room. A shower seems ideal to get the smoke smell from her clothes.

As she enters the room, the smile leaves her face. Jennifer's comments rattled her. It brought her back to her mother and the reason she was a single parent. The questions she had asked and never answered reared their heads again. Maddi sighs as she enters the shower. On impulse, she pulls the shower cap from her hair. The water flows slowly and soothingly over her hair and body. She turns her face to the spray and lets it cascade over her body. Slowly, she washes her hair and then grabs her shower gel. The gentle scent gives her that good feeling.

After her shower, she blots the extra water from her hair, deciding to forgo her blow-dryer and let it air-dry. She sighs and moves toward the window. The night sky's translucent gleam with the last remnant of the dying sun gave a warming glow. Sunset seems to continue longer tonight. She looks longingly at the sky, hoping for answers. It seems like her luck ran out, and the old insecurities and questions rear their monstrous heads. She had always wondered about her father's family. What of his parents, or were they as stuffy as her maternal grandparents? Why would grandparents not want to know their grandchild? Or was Verne estranged from his family, and her mother was a secret?

With the old thoughts looming large and frightening, she wanted to run. She would go to bed, and tomorrow would go to her old home in Brooklyn. There in the old home, just maybe, she can maintain some balance. If she were honest, she is running. She needs the solace and comfort of her home. She needs peace.

Maddi slept fitfully the night before. It was not surprising she had nightmares. She must remember to thank her dear aunt Jennifer.

At breakfast, she told her father her desire to visit her old home. He looked concerned, wanting to know why. She explained her mother's things were still there. Later, her aunt Carol, uncle Fitzroy, and her grandparents would meet and decide what to do with her things. She did not tell him Aunt Carol lived in the same house, that it was a mother-daughter house. Her sudden departure from Brooklyn precluded making any plans as to what to do with her mother's things.

Her father suggested she call all the parties and make a date rather than go there first. Maddi knew it made sense, but she wanted to be alone. She called her three school pals Pam, Joan, and Phil. Well, he wants to take her. She will release her secret weapon: Pam. This made her smile. He forgot it was a temporary truce for the visit of Jennifer and Will. This ongoing vacillation of feelings was suffocating her. She wants her mother back. She wants how it was before.

As tears pricked the back of her lids, she closed her eyes, bowing her head. For the umpteenth time, she asked why her mother left her. *Oh, mother,* she thought, *things are so complicated.* There are so many questions. Her paternal grandparents were weird. She felt there was a story there.

Maddi called and made the arrangements. Her father insisted he would take her; no need for the bus. She wondered why the insistence. She looked at him, and he suddenly loomed like a mountain, big and imposing. She agreed and told Phoebe.

On Wednesday, she kissed Jan goodbye reluctantly and headed for Brooklyn. Jan started to cry. Maddi was upset. Phoebe held Jan as she started after them. The other children left for camp an hour earlier. Maddi did not like seeing Jan cry. She became a little morose as they started off. "She will be fine. Phoebe will distract her, and soon, she will be laughing again. Most likely, she will go for a ride. Jan enjoys that. She will be smiling and waving to everyone. I see you don't believe me, but call when you get to Brooklyn. Call and see," he ended.

Maddi did not answer. She just wants to get to Brooklyn and have time alone, meet with her friends, and then look through her mother's drawers, papers, clothes. Her mother had several dance costumes from earlier recitals and music sheets, albums, and other couture clothes. She knew years ago she did not possess her mother's flair for clothes or to wear them with sophistication as her mother did. Her mother was extremely beautiful, and several portraits were a testament to that. She sighed, not really wanting to do what she was going to do. She knew of a family that waited five years, and it did not get any easier. She remembered one daughter saying it was the worst decision to wait. The pain was not any less. "Get it over and done with," she had said. There were five of them, and she believed they should know.

"What are you going to do while I go through my mother's things? My three friends are going to meet me there. The relatives will be there in the evening," Madison said.

"Oh, Madison, that is too much for a child to do. I am going to be there for moral support. I am not sure you would want your friends there with your aunt, uncle, and grandparents. I made a vow. I will never be apart from you again even if hell bars the way!" he ended vehemently.

Maddi jerked her head at his tone. Not for the first time, it crossed her mind he'd be a formidable enemy. She eyed him out of the corner of her eye with her brows up. He must have noticed because he said, "See that? That is typical Joyce. I do not know anyone who can do that. You look just like her."

"Really, Dad? I thought I looked like you. I gave you my face," she mimicked.

"Yes, daughter, I did, and I would not have it any other way today, but I'm not talking about the physical. I'm talking about character traits, idiosyncrasies, little things peculiar to that person. You inherited that, and it makes me happy. In the perfect life, I would want you to look like your mother, but for practical purposes, it might as well be what it is; it makes life easier," he said softly.

"Did you love her, really and truly love her? Would you have married her if the war had not happened?" she asked, her voice strained with emotions.

"As sure as the sun rises in the east and sets in the west. I never envisioned marrying anyone else until her parents told me she had moved on and was dating some doctor, while omitting the most crucial information: I have a daughter. Can you imagine how cruel that is? All this time, I'm mourning a lost love, and my child is growing without a father. Why? What did I do to earn their hatred?"

"Nothing except to get their daughter pregnant out of wedlock. They are Christians, and they teach their children the sanctity of marriage, biblical responsibility of remaining chaste until their wedding night. You made a mockery of their teaching. You represent what they dislike in modern living."

"That may be true, but what of you? You are innocent, my darling, and that is what I find so hard to fathom. For the sake of forgiveness, couldn't they relent for you? What sort of God holds children accountable for the deeds of their parents? No, daughter. No, I do not understand that."

For the first time, Madison thought of the impact it would have had finding out you are a father. His feelings, she did not consider. For a proud man, it would be humiliating if he really loved her mom as he said he did!

"So how did you and my mother meet?" She knew how but needed to hear from him to check the facts.

He told her about being hospitalized, and she helped him to recover. The nurses were tired of his dour attitude and implacable personality. Sunshine walked in his room one day, and thus began the turning point. Her mother—soft, warm, and funny—coaxed a smile from him. She told him she missed a genuine Kodak moment, shaking her head. She told him it was not true. He had a face only a mother would love. He laughed so hard the nurses crowded his room to see if he was having a nervous breakdown. "Were you?" she asked softly.

"Were you what?" he asked, frowning.

"Having a nervous breakdown?" she asked mischievously.

"No, Madison, I was doing something else. Do you want to know?"

"Sure."

"I was busy falling in love with her. I was surprised she did not have a steady boyfriend, as beautiful as she was. I could not wait to be discharged, and therein, my real healing started. I wanted to see her outside of the confines of the hospital.

"We started dating. I lived in Park Slope, and when she was not doing auditions, giving private dance lessons, and working at Lorna's Dance Studio, she was on dates with me. Things were hectic, but we made it work. Time spent together was precious, and time spent apart infused a desperate longing. I was so happy that about six weeks after discharge, I took her to see my parents. I wanted them to meet the love of my life. We were to have dinner with my parents."

Madison turns and faces him. She is intrigued by his story. "You did? So what happened?" her voice breathless.

"Oh, boy! My mother—or parents—invited an old girlfriend, Veronica. We dated while we were in high school and had when I first enlisted in the army. I'd never told the parents about the accident that landed me in the hospital, and except for James and Amina, no one else knew. Furthermore, I minimized its importance so they would not come to see me in the hospital. James and Amina were listed as contacts and next of kin should anything go awry. So we went, and it was awkward.

"Mother made sure Joyce knew who she preferred, placing Veronica at my left and Dad at the right. She tried to exclude Joyce from the conversation. At times, I had to bring the conversation to neutral grounds so all could participate.

"By then, I was fuming. I asked my mother why she invited Veronica. She said something about healthy competition. You mean excluding her from the conversation and talking about things she could not possibly know? I told her Veronica was history and took leave shortly after.

"It was the first time Joyce was mad with me. She wanted to know what kind of viper's den I set for her. I tried to reassure her, but she was not buying it. She lapsed into silence all the way to Brooklyn. I apologized, but she did not answer.

"As we exited the Brooklyn Bridge, I found a florist and bought her a dozen red roses. I got a wan smile. I knew she had this weakness for pistachio ice cream. That did the trick. I was almost forgiven."

Madison started to laugh. He knew Joyce. That was her weakness. She had used that bribe also.

"So we went to my apartment, and I turned the stereo on. I put on the iceman Jerry Butler, "For Your Precious Love." We waltzed to that rich, romantic song, and romantic it was. It was the first time we ever—"

"Stop! Delicate ears, eh? Do you realize I am still a child? Do you think you should reveal all that?" she said indignantly.

"I am sorry, Madison. I was carried away with my memories. Your mannerisms are so alike even now."

"I can tell you got carried away, but know I am not that curious about the intimate details of your relationship with my mother."

He apologized for his lapse, but it set Maddi thinking about his marriage to Phoebe. *He is lucky*, she mused. In his life, he finds two women who love him, and some people cannot find one. Her mother loved him. She never married, and Maddi never accepted fully her reason for not marrying. She is aware of the pedophiles preying on stepchildren. She is aware of incestuous relations. Bad people are everywhere. She believes her mother never gave herself a chance because she was in love with a dead man. The fact he is alive now has little bearing on her decision back then, even if she believes he was her true love.

Chapter 6

Soon, they reached East Eighty-Seventh Street. As it was midmorning, the parking was easy. She walks upstairs and unlocks the front door. She opens the windows in the living room, kitchen, and bathroom. She opens the refrigerator door, and there is water, juice, cheese, butter, grapes, cantaloupe, cabbage, and carrots. In the freezer, there is bacon, Brown 'N Serve sausages, chicken legs, a whole chicken, fish, frozen vegetables, and ice cream.

"Inside is just a wee bit musty," Maddi said, "but Aunt Carol opens it up every other day or so to eliminate any stale odor. There is water or juice if you like. What do you think you would like to eat for dinner? There's chicken leg and whole chicken, salmon, and kingfish. We eat mostly poultry and fish. We can thaw it in the sink, and maybe we can prevent Aunt Carol from cooking this evening. However, you get first choice. Auntie is not fussy."

"How about me cooking? Your friends are coming, right? So let me cook while you young 'uns do what you do once I give them the once-over."

"Give what kind of once-over?"

The doorbell chimed, and he muttered under his breath, "Saved by the bell." He moved toward the kitchen to raid the refrigerator. He takes out the legs and removes the cabbage and carrots. All the ingredients are present for stir-fry chicken. He puts the chicken in an aluminum bowl and fills it with water. He gets a cutting board and rests it on the counter. The knives in the dish drainer are dull. He remembers a file in his toolbox. It's easy to fetch so he can sharpen the knives—the chef knife and the paring knife.

He hears the greetings of teenagers, the squeals and instant chatter. A voice tells Maddi it is high time she returns to Brooklyn and how much she is missed. "You are not the only one missing Maddi. We all are, right, Phil?"

That was his cue: Phil indeed. He enters the room, and one very bright-eyed girl gasped, "Oh my god!"

The others look up, seeing Verne standing with a makeshift apron. "Sweet Mary and Joseph on a Friday. Oh my god. This is not real. Our Father who art in heaven, holy be your name. Lord of mercy, how could this be? You look so alike. Do you not frighten yourselves?" said Pam, hands crossed over her breast.

One thing Maddi did not consider is the effect her resemblance may have on her friends. Phil's and Joan's eyes bulging with mouths agape is truly a picturesque moment. Maddi is amused by their reaction. "Thank you, Pam, for always bringing the drama. You have your finger on the pulse. You are a rare gift, my friend. Now that that is out of the way, it's time for some formal introductions. This is my dad. Dad, meet Pam, Joan, and Phil, friends from grade school," said Maddi, introducing the trio to her father.

He comes fully into the room, shakes their hands, and tells them he is happy to meet them. He removes the towel from his waist and tells Maddi he is getting something from his car. After he leaves, there is silence, then Phil remarks, clearing his throat. "Wow, that's your father? He is a big guy. What does he do? Those hands are very muscular. I would not want to tangle with those for any reason."

"No reason you should. He is CDR. Verne Moodie. He builds and repairs bikes, cars, rail ramps. He is happy putting to use those muscles helping the little old ladies in the community."

"That is so cool," said Joan. "So what is it like in Mount Vernon? Is there much to do? I hear about some big hill there. It sort of dissociates itself from NY, having its own mayor. Is it very big?"

"Bless you. You are informed. It is not Brooklyn, not as hectic. It is a slower pace but nice. The usual amenities are there: shopping, sightseeing, zoo, trails for riding, historic landmarks, and the like. Transportation is different, but there is Metro-North. It is not far from the Bronx, and the iron horse is next door."

While they are laughing, Verne comes in with a file. The gadget looks strange, and Pam asks what it is and what it is used for. Verne answers politely with a smile. He asks if they are staying for a while. The three visitors look uncomfortable. Maddi turns to him with angry eyes, and he explains he is going to cook and wants to know if they would like to stay. Relief shows on their faces. They assure him they are in no rush and will stay. He walks to the kitchen. As he leaves, Pam asks, "How old is he?"

"Too old for you, plus he is married."

Pam, undeterred, asks, "Does he have a younger brother, single, unattached, just as gorgeous? Mmm. He is a dish. I would say eat your heart out, Fabio. Girl, your dad is fine—fine in capitals, fine."

"You know, Pam, you are outrageous as ever. That's Maddi's father!" said Joan in exasperation.

"Well, he is not a monk. Oh well, I can dream, can't I? If ever there is or was a hunk, he gets my vote."

"Every handsome man gets your vote, Pam!"

They laugh. When Pam is in the man-crazy mood, there is no stopping her. They discuss the semester that ended. Maddi prefers to listen to the debate raging. She offers them refreshments of crackers and cheese and apple juice. She puts this on the dining table, grabs a cracker, and goes to sit in the adjoining living room.

Phil walks over and sits on the handle, ruffling her hair. She tilts her head back and looks at him. "I really miss you. You do not return calls, and you do not call. I know it has been trying, but I want to know what you are feeling. Maybe I can help. Ever thought of that? You find some other guy up in Mount Vernon?" he said ever so softly to preclude the other two. He drops a kiss on her nose and brushes his lips lightly across her own. He eases her along the couch and turns toward her.

Maddi sinks into the sofa so that her head rests on his shoulder. She likes Phil and at one time believed she could love him, but uncertainty is an exacting force, so she is unsure.

"Hey, you two, what gives? No hanky-panky, not with Papa in the kitchen. Remember, he just sharpened the knife," said Pam.

"Thank you, Pam. I do not know what I would do without you," said Maddi as she turns in Phil's arms and offers a conciliatory kiss.

Phil accepts the gesture with gladness. She moves from his arms as the phone rings. She speaks with Aunt Carol. Tyler and Zach are on an overnight trip, and Jada will go to babysit her cousin by her aunt Jean and stay over so she and her husband would enjoy their anniversary.

Tantalizing smells rush into the living room. Whatever her father is cooking is kicking outside. She puts her hand up and walks to the kitchen. Her father, humming, turns toward her with a smile. "Can I help? Something sure smells good in here. What are you making again?"

"Stir-fried chicken. So it is bothering your nose? Glad to know. Heaven knows I have been trying to coax some good flavors into this chicken and out of the seasoning. Thanks, but I'm good."

"You know, for a soldier, you do not eat heavy. I am surprised at that."

"Well, Madison, if you are not working, then it does not make sense, plus when we go on survival training, it's minimal food, and you eat off the land. Anyway, I chow down plenty. My metabolism burns it off quickly, and I bike and exercise regularly. No middle-aged spread or beer gut for me."

"Would you consider going back in the military?"

"At one time, I considered it, but I changed my mind for personal reasons," he said as he sees her raised eyebrows. It's as if he could see in her mind.

Maddi exhales slowly, unaware until then she is holding her breath. "Okay, Chef Verne, I leave you to it. If it tastes as good as it smells, it's a home run."

Verne smiles at his daughter. The resemblance is remarkable even to him. What a gift Joyce gave him, knowing there would be repercussions but doing it anyway. What a sacrifice!

As Madison walks into the living room, she cautions herself not to fall under the spell of the great Verne Moodie even if he is her father. From her friends' reaction, no explanation of who fathered her is necessary. "My father needs no help, so no kitchen duty. Just want to say thanks, guys, for not holding my silence against me and being morose. It is getting better. It was strange at first, meeting my father and stepmother and four children, but I tell you they are the coolest kids I've ever seen. And Phoebe, his wife, is not Cinderella's stepmother. She is so sweet. They really make me feel welcome."

"I, for one, am glad it is working out for you. You are too nice a person for things not to go right for you. I just wish that I could've spared you even a little of the heartache. You know I love you, sis," said Joan as she walks over and hugs Madison.

"Don't get maudlin," Maddi said. "Pam, what about the Italian Adonis you were sweet on?"

"Chile. Had to cut that fool loose. We went out for a while, as you know, but he had this notion that I either owe him something or I have something for him. One night, get all dressed up, dinner, and movie. Never mind snuggling in the movie and a snatch kiss here and there, so when we reach home, the man decided to treat me like a peep show. You know these houses in Canarsie close by, so I guess a kiss goodnight was in order, but no. That was not enough. One hell of a wrestling match to get him off me. I never knew one man could have so many hands. Turned out he was a wrestler who is an octopus as well. And you know, the food never tastes that good anyway, and the movie not that good. Yes, had to fight for my chastity. By the time I got away, I was disheveled, angry, and sweating. Couldn't even get to return the dress to Macy's the next day."

By this time, Madison, Joan, and Phil are cracking up. They laugh hard and long. Pam reluctantly joins in. Madison laughs so hard, tears stream down her cheeks. Now she knows why she can never do without Pam. Pam makes her laugh as crazy as she makes all of them at times.

"How many hands did what's-his-name have?" Maddi asked. She is grateful for the time she is spending with the three of them.

Her father comes to the door to announce the meal is hot and waiting for everyone to eat. Madison goes in the kitchen, rinses the plates and utensils, takes them to the dining table, and her father brings the pot with the stir-fry chicken and a bowl of rice. They hold hands and say grace. Commander smiles and asks what the laughing was about. Maddi smiles and said Pam was recounting her last date.

"Really! You don't say. It sounded hilarious if the laughter I heard was any indication," he said.

"Well, Mr. Verne, can I call you that? I went out with this guy—dinner, movie, and home. This fool believed that because he bought dinner and paid for the movie, he should collect when we got home, if you know what I mean. The man was an animal, hands all over. It was WrestleMania. I had to wrestle my way from his car to keep my dignity. He had all hands. If I had time, I would've counted them all. I only got up to six because I was so busy fighting. Do you know the commercial with the pink octopus vacuuming, ironing, dusting, and a multitude of things? He was no better, so many hands on one body."

The laughter continues long after the tale. The relief is exactly what she needs. It is also a welcome distraction from her evening project. She has reservations about going through her mom's clothes and personal items. It is going to be painful, but the jovial atmosphere earlier should ease the arduous task. She knows she cannot delude herself.

About two hours later, her friends left. She enters her mother's room with bravado, with Pam's tale of her Italian ex-boyfriend. Each time she remembers Pam's description, she laughs. She opens her mother's closet where she has a cedar box. This has costumes. She then looks at the bedhead with its multiple compartments. The night tables are attached. She pulls a book tied with a ribbon from the back. Opening this, it seems like a diary. Madison feels self-conscious about reading her mother's diary. She has so many questions about her father and their meeting and eventual intimacy that brought her into the world that she is overcome with curiosity. There are two photo albums, which surprisingly show no signs of yellowing due to age, yet they must be old.

Gingerly, she opens the beige and brown album. Inscribed inside, she sees "To Verne. Love, Joyce." She puts her hand to her mouth. When did her mother do this? She seems to be learning new things every step of the way. She is sorry she let timidity stop her from asking more questions. What shall she do? She cannot not give him the album, but what if it causes problems with Phoebe? This is one adult world she wants no part of.

She opens the second, and it says, "Madison." Leafing through, she sees her baby picture staring back at her. The pictures chronicle her life, it seems. Maybe she did the same for Verne. The old stir of resentment stirs in her breast. Just when she believes they reach a level of understanding, then this crops up. Conflicting thoughts flow through her mind, and with a massive sigh, she gets up with the album and takes it to her father. She hands it to him silently, all the while, resentment claws at her breast. He accepts the album, and she averts her eyes. Tears well in her eyes. So much for bravery! She walks back to the room. She has no desire to look at the album. She prays he asks her no questions. She smiles grimly. Even if she ate his food, so what?

Madison picks up the book with the ribbon. If it's time to cry, she might as well get an early start. Soon, she is so engrossed in its contents, she loses track of time. Her mother was a brilliant writer. It was soft, poignant, uncomplicated, and poetic—a woman's immortal words for the man she loves, her forever love. The pictures painted were vivid and romantic: their trips to Central Park lying in the grass while he serenaded her with "Open Arms" by Journey and Rita Coolidge's "We're All Alone." She's on her back, and he is bending over her, singing all those love songs, which end in his kissing her. They hugged, laughed, and talked. They made plans to marry and start a family in another two years or so.

Lost in her mother's love story, she is unprepared for the September 1990 entry. Her mother met Verne's parents. His parents were snobs and inhospitable. She was happy when the meal was over, and they left Mount Vernon. That night, they had their first quarrel as he dared to defend and make light of their horrible behavior. It was the night of many firsts.

Red roses, ice cream, soft romantic music, and a room lit with only the streetlights conspired that night, and they became one. They fused their passion in the most elementary of ways as men and women often did. Once the line was crossed, there was no going back. They had tasted, and now they thirsted. It was not a thirst that would easily quench with a sip or a glass. It would take a lifetime of drinking to assuage that thirst and at best was iffy. Their love became a raging inferno. Each waltz or dance was a preamble to their lovemaking. One of their favorites was "Chariots of Fire." Wrapped in each other's arms, it seemed like a natural progression of things. Her days spanned auditions or part-time dance instructor and Verne's lover by night, where she sank blissfully into oblivion.

She is fascinated and cannot stop reading now. Heartbreak follows the euphoria as he was called back to active duty. The Gulf War started in 1989. He went away in November 1990. He left behind Joyce and a barely conceived Madison. Joyce learned that he died in a land mine accident. Pregnant and devastated, she visited his parents. His mother was skeptical about her pregnancy. She asked Verne's mother to let her know when his body was returned, especially for the memorial service, so that his unborn child would know of his father's sacrifice. His mother told her she would take the baby and raise him. She would adopt him and would even compensate her. The asterisks indicated her mother's feelings.

Madison starts sobbing as if her heart would break. Her father enters with a frown on his face. Seeing her crumpled on the bed, he wraps his arms around her. She is too broken to resist. She just cries and cries. Verne holds her close, rocking her and kissing her hair. She does not pull away but sobs until there are only sniffles.

As her tears dry, she remains in her father's arms. She lies there, reluctant to move. He seems content to hold her. "You okay, sweetheart?"

She doesn't answer, just raises her shoulders. She is not concerned about meeting her maternal grandparents, Uncle Fitzroy, or Aunt Carol. She understands now why her mother was so cagey about certain questions and answers she gave. Now she knows why she never talked about her paternal grandparents. Did they imagine her mother would sell her baby and walk away? They must have poor opinions of people in general if they think that would ever happen. Who did they think they were?

Before long, the doorbell rings, and it is Uncle Fitz. Her father opens the door, and Madison hears, "Wow, oh man, oh man."

By the time she drags herself to the living room, both men introduced themselves, shaking hands and bumping shoulders. "Hi, Maddi, my favorite niece. How are yah? It is good to see you," he said, hugging her.

She hugs him back and mumbles okay.

"Don't tell me I am the first one here. You've been crying, sweetie. What is the matter?" asked Fitz.

"Oh, Uncle, it was so wrong for my mother to die and leave me. I feel so unhappy at times. I am learning I have a father who has a family, a father I believed had died in a land mine accident, so I feel as if I am tossed in raging water, and I am thrashing about. I have all these conflicting emotions, like did my father come to look for my mother after he came back from the war? And where was he all this time? My mother wants me to get to know him, to give him a chance because he is a great guy, and I want to. I cannot disappoint my mother. Now I am finding out how much she sacrificed for me, and I am mad. Now my dad is such a sensation to everyone because I look so much like him without the moustache."

"Come here!" He hugs her closer.

"Take it easy. It is a learning experience for both of you. You are a good kid and will do the right thing. You are not mean. It is a lot to digest all at once. You do not have to do this all alone. I believe your dad understands. But seriously, the way you two look alike is uncanny. So happy you don't have a moustache. Could be worse. He can't deny you, and he doesn't look as if he wants to. Give yourself time, dumpling. I am sorry I never met him. I believe we could've been great friends," he said, kissing the top of her head.

Meanwhile, her father's features remain neutral. He inhales and looks through the window. He inhales sharply and declares, "They are here." He walks to the front door and opens it to Ethel and Benjamin Brookes, her grandparents.

Their eyes bulge as they enter. Actually, it looks more like fright, and she wonders why. Her grandmother's "oh" and hands to her mouth she considers strange, but the terror on her grandfather's face says it all. She follows the stare, and it alights on her father. He seems as if carved in bronze, nose flaring, eyes snapping, and mouth tight as he looks at them. Madison gapes at her father's face, fascinated and terrified simultaneously. She is happy the look is not hers.

"Oh god, what have we done? Lord, forgive me!" her grandfather said, making the sign of the cross. Her grandparents react to the identical look of her and her father. She closes her eyes, shaking her head. Her father starts toward them with fists clenched, barely self-controlled. Madison is reminded of a leopard getting ready to pounce, gaze not wavering.

"Mr. and Mrs. Brooke, I see you remember me. How many years has it been, fifteen, sixteen? Why don't you tell your granddaughter how you know me? See, she does not believe I came back to look for her mother, that I did not care that I walked away because every responsible man who is intimate with a woman must return to see if there is an aftermath."

"We are sorry. We have to go," her grandfather said and, grabbing her grandmother's hand, exits the apartment.

Fitz follows, asking them to wait. "What is going on?"

She could hear his voice but not the conversation. Verne walks toward her with arms outstretched. She walks into them. She is shocked, but there are no tears left. She is numb. Nothing is going as planned. Today is supposed to be a relaxing day, where she refreshes and regroups, but the plans go awry. She hugs her father because she does not know what else to do. She feels like a crybaby also. She wonders if Aunt Carol will come and if anything can be saved.

She looks at her father's watch. It is six twenty. She feels obligated to wait and see her aunt. She will go to her room and pack some more clothes and personal effects. Her mother was a Mary Kay addict and had everything Mary Kay: foundation, mineral powder, body wash, perfume, lipstick, lip gloss, cleaners, moisturizers, and color cosmetics. These she will certainly not waste. Her mother had flawless skin, no signs of aging, and she attributed this to Mary Kay skincare. She smiles in remembrance as she could see her mom apply Downtown Brown lipstick. She was gorgeous.

"Thank you. I will go pack some clothes and personal effects. My mother's room is for another day even if Auntie comes home now. Auntie lives downstairs, so I will not be inconveniencing her. All desire to sort through papers, clothes, things is lost. We can leave the rest of the food for Auntie and Uncle and you if you need seconds," said Maddi.

Forcing herself, she walks with all the energy she has and takes a duffel bag from her closet. She randomly selects clothes from her closet and chest of drawers, not interested in whether they fit or not. Except for the clothes Phoebe bought her, everything else she has is from the year before. She makes the effort to find three dresses without spaghetti straps. Suddenly, she wants to get away. She empties the Mary Kay products into a tote and, calling her father, tells him she is ready to go.

"Not so fast. Aren't you waiting for your aunt?" he asked.

"It is almost seven o'clock. I do not have the energy anymore. I wish she…," her voice tapering off. "Please, I have to go." Her voice and eyes are tearful, and he nods, taking up the duffel bag. She scribbles a note for her aunt to leave under her door.

As she straightens, her aunt's car pulls up. Uncle Brad, an affable man, gets out and opens the door for her. Madison is greeted by hugs, and her aunt sizes up the situation. "Too much, eh? I understand. It is okay. Just take care of yourself. We are not going anywhere. Anytime you are up to it is fine. Nice to see you again, Mr. Moodie. My husband, Brad," she said.

Maddi looks at Brad's expression and bursts out laughing. He looks like a cartoon character that is surprised, his eyebrows touching his hairline. Her father's smile seems genuine as he shakes Brad's hand. "I guess it's a cliché now. You got me there. Did not expect that one," he said, still looking from Maddi to Verne. He acknowledged he is the culprit for the latter.

"It is okay. Like Auntie says, it is not going anywhere. I can come again. Zach, Tyler, and Jada may be home then. I will be happy to see them. Give them my best." She hugs them and walks to the car.

Verne says goodbye, and they are on their way. He asks her preference for a radio station, and when she shrugs, he tunes in to CBS FM. She consoles herself that it is easy listening, and it precludes conversation. She could feel his glance on her several times, but she keeps her silence. What a mess! She feels as if she is a part of a soap opera. How can one death cause so much upheaval? If this is adulthood, then others are welcome to it. I can live without them.

They continue in silence for some time, each lost in private thoughts as the car eats up the miles. "Madison, it is going to be okay," Verne said softly. "It doesn't seem that way now, but in time, you will gain and learn from it. That is part of growing pains. You go to bed and wake up, and the world is different. It changed without notice. Yours is more dramatic and brash because it is coming at you all at once. It can be frightening. One of mankind's greatest needs is comfort and security, that feeling of well-being, but once challenged can throw you in a tailspin like you expressed today. No one is judging you. Take your time and assimilate the newness gradually. I am here to help you. I want to help. Try and find it in your heart to forgive me for not being there at birth and your growing years. You are not alone. Never think you are alone or that you have to figure this out all by yourself."

As he stops talking, she looks at him. She notices his face in the lengthening shadows of the evening tide. He is incredibly handsome. His features are near perfect: nose, eyes, cheekbones with slight hollows in the cheeks, clearly defined lips, and that incredible cleft in his chin. He wears his look well, yet she does not see or sense conceit in him. She begins to see why her mother was so stuck on him. Frankly, the picture she had of him did not do him justice, yet those Phoebe took were more accurate.

During her contemplation of his features, he turns and sees her looking at him. "What?"

"Nothing," she says with a smile. "Well, I am acknowledging why my mom was so hung up on you. You know she met many men in her job—doctors, physical therapists, pharmaceutical reps, technicians, businessmen—and they never seemed to stir her. She dated this doctor once for about a year. He was crazy about her, but not mom! Oh, I am very fond of Richard, but, darling, he's not the one, so I coined the term NVSE. Thankfully, there were not many prospects."

"NVSE? Okay, what does that mean?" he asked, amused.

"It means Not Verne's Standard of Excellence."

"What?" His laugh, rich and powerful, fills the car. "You really are my kid. You could never come up with a term like that unless you are related to me."

"Well, I am your daughter," she says with a shrug.

"Yes, you are," he said softly, reaching for her hand.

Sometime later, a gentle voice said softly, "Maddi, wake up. We are home."

Disoriented, she opens her eyes, and they are in Mount Vernon. She yawns and stretches. The sun had set, and remnants of gold and purple lingered. Maddi gets out with her bag and tote. Phoebe is at the door with Jan. Maddi vaguely notices another car as she bends to kiss Jan. "Of course, I am stale turnips!" Maddi turns and hugs Phoebe with a smile. Jan wants Maddi to take her, so she shifts her bag to her left shoulder and takes her in her right hand. "That is gratitude for you. She cried after you left, then we became friends. Hugs and kisses all day, and in ten seconds, puff, all that is gone. Maddi is here. Look at her, not even repentant," said Phoebe.

Jan nods her head as if she understands her mother's complaint.

"Is that them, darling?" a voice asks from inside. By this, her father is kissing Phoebe.

"Verne, darling, your mother-in-law is here. Showed up as usual, not needing an appointment to see her grandchildren and son-in-law."

He seems unconcerned. Arms around Phoebe, he calls out. "Is my favorite mother-in-law in the house?"

A pretty lady with salt-and-pepper hair comes hustling into the room. "Verne!"

He hugs her and kisses her cheek. "Hello, Maggie, so good to see you. Where is Percy?"

Before she can answer, Percy comes from the back, arms out to shake Verne's hand. Both men greet each other warmly. "Oh, dear, you must be Madison. Honey, I could not wait to meet my new granddaughter," said Maggie.

Madison barely has time to hand Jan to Phoebe and put the bags on the floor before she is caught in an all-encompassing hug. Madison feels the tears prick her eyes. The warmth of her embrace and warmth of her personality reaches Madison as kindred spirits. Maddi returns the hug. "Thank you, Grandma," she said impulsively.

"I feel like an excess," said Phoebe, "but, Madison, that is my mother, Maggie, and my father, Percy Thornton."

"Oh, Phoebe, why so formal? Oh, dear, we have to put a little bit more meat on you. Phoebe, you're not feeding this child? Never mind. I'll take care of that. Madison, honey, I know you had a rough spell, but it will get better. God takes care of His own. Weeping endures for the night, but joy comes in the morning," Maggie quotes from the Bible.

Percy gives Madison a bear hug. Madison is amazed by Phoebe's parents. They are warm and friendly. They are the antithesis of her maternal grandparents. Daniel and the twins run in and greet Madison. Maggie asks if either Verne or Madison is hungry. They confess they've eaten dinner but are up for dessert. Maggie seems delighted. "Do I have a treat for you? I have pecan pie, cherry pie, chocolate chip cookies, and Greek cookies."

Verne looks at Madison. "Ladies first!" Madison hesitates briefly, then asks for pecan pie and a Greek cookie. She had fond memories of Greek cookies, eating them with her mom. Somehow, it seems all right to eat them without her mom. Reluctantly, she refuses the pistachio and chocolate ice cream. She does not like chocolate ice cream or chocolate chip cookies. She smiles as she remembers the strange looks she got when she told Joan she did not like chocolate beyond hot cocoa.

Her father asks for both pies minus the cookies. "Oh, Dad! Really? I slaved all day baking these cookies just for you. Right, Grandma?" Daniel said with a mock hurt look.

"Okay, just one. Which one do you recommend? Never mind. I will have the Greek cookie."

So both father and daughter eat the pie then the cookie. Suddenly, Madison realizes it is very quiet. She looks up, and all eight pairs of eyes are fastened on them. "What?" she asked.

"Honey, you eat like your father. It is fascinating looking at both of you. It is like looking at one or the other in a double flick. Phoebe is right. You can substitute heads and never know the difference, but I would. No matter what they say, if you look like your father, you will be lucky. It's an old saying," Maggie said, kissing Madison on the head.

Madison smiles but feels self-conscious. To ease the tension, Verne picks up Jan and says, "See!"

That caused everyone to laugh. Now the attention shifts, and Madison joins the laughter. All's well that ends well, the adage pops into her head. Thank goodness she likes Phoebe's parents. Maggie shoos them out and into the family room for games. Maddi and her father finish eating dessert, rinsing the plates and forks, and wipe the counter before heading to join the others. Jan quickly runs to Maddi, and she picks her up. Jan laughs, clapping her chubby hands. Maddi starts to bounce Jan up and down as she walks around the room.

As she walks by Percy, he stretches to ruffle Jan's hair. "Hey, beauty, do you have a hug for your favorite grandfather?" said Percy.

"Yes."

Maddi bends over, and Jan goes to her grandfather. She frames Percy's face with her hands, smiling at him. Jan throws her head back and laughs. She is such a happy baby!

Maddi uses the opportunity to slip away. She wants to go lie down, but she remembers the pie and cookie sitting in her stomach. It is not even half an hour since that pie! Her bed is shouting, "Come to me!"

Just this once, she will answer and go to bed. She finds Phoebe with her father in the living room and bids them good night, pleading tiredness.

Maddi skips a bath, thinking humorously that dirt will only hurt if it falls on you, so she is going to bed. She inhales and exhales for about five minutes to center herself. She is looking for a good night's sleep despite the events of the day. Emptying her mind, she turns out the light and pulls a light sheet over her legs. She drifts off.

Her rest is fitful. In her dream, she is with her mother at Prospect Park. They are listening to music under a magnolia tree. She is humming a song Madison does not know. She picks up their picnic basket and places sandwiches and chicken on a tablecloth. As they eat, her mother becomes quiet and stares off into the distance. "What are you thinking, Mom?" she asked.

Her mother looks sheepish and says, "Verne."

"Golly gee, Mom! What a surprise," she said sarcastically, rolling her eyes. "Will you ever forget him? It's been more than sixteen years already. What was he lined with, gold or platinum? That is obsession. It is abnormal."

"It is not as if he left. He went to war. That is why war is ugly. Too many people get hurt on both sides. But Verne was and is my forever love. We loved each other deeply, and how could I not love him? Look what he gave me: you. I would not change that in a million years. Some people live and never experience love, but I have. See, daughter, you are his gift to me," her mother said.

Her mother disappears from her mind, and she is walking on Flatlands Avenue toward her grandparents' home. She is walking with purpose; she has some home truths to tell that pair. How could they subject her to a life without a father? Are they that unforgiving? Parents rant and rave when their daughters get pregnant as teenagers. Her mother was in her twenties, an adult, for heaven's sake.

She lengthens her strides as her blood boils at their meanness. She takes the keys from her bag and enters the house. "Grandma, Grandpa, I need to speak with you. Where are you?" Impatient in tone and arrogant in voice as she bellows for them. She sees them. They are sitting on the back patio with fruit juice, not that she cares.

"I need to talk with both of you now. What kind of a sentence did you place on me, and for what crime? How can you do this to me and live so piously, toting a bag of Bibles to church three times per week? What, you lose some pages, like the part that says forgive seventy times seven, eh?" By this, her voice is getting louder and louder, and her grandparents try to shush her.

From a distance, she hears, "Madison, wake up! Wake up, Madison." Arms are on her shoulders, shaking her awake. "Madison, you are shouting in your sleep," Phoebe said softly. "Are you okay, honey? I can get some warm milk with honey for you."

"No, thank you. I'll be all right now. Hope I didn't wake everyone," she said guiltily.

The rest of her night is uneventful, even if it took a while to get back to sleep. The next morning, there is a lot of energy as the children vote to stay home with their grandparents. Madison has little time to brood or be depressed. Between the phone calls, she is now back in the loop with the old gang, and Maggie's outrageous energy has everyone hopping. Jan remains her constant companion but seems to enjoy her grandfather's arms too. Maggie has a baking team, a cooking team, and a cleanup crew. Madison finds it easier to go along with Maggie. She is permanently deaf to opposition, something Percy acknowledges. With all the extra activities, Madison admits she will find less time to brood. The children really enjoy their grandmother, and vice versa. The love, the caring, and the friendship in the family are clear to an onlooker.

As she is sipping lemonade, Phoebe says how great her mother is and that she loves her a lot, but she's a hurricane. She just causes upheavals, good intentions though they are. She spoils all the children rotten, and by the time she leaves, she has the task of reestablishing her boundaries for all the children. She ends that she loves her mother but cannot live with her for very long.

Madison hugs her and tells her not to worry; after all, she lives with Verne. Phoebe laughs, shooing her away. She looks at Madison, shaking her head, stating here she is believing that Madison is on her side. Madison shrugs, unrepentant. Madison enters the kitchen, and she hears strains of Bach. That is one of her favorites.

She inhales deeply as the music flows into her, and that beautifully written music flows to meet her. She closes her eyes as "Jesus, Joy of Man's Desiring" wafts through the air, and she is caught. Unconsciously, she starts to sing, and the melody pushes from her lungs, her heart, her head. It could not stop as she loses herself in the melody, and she sings as if it is her last song. Tears stream from her face as she finishes to an audience of everyone present. She hears the applause and wonders at it.

"Madison, darling, that is wonderful! It is like Leontyne Price. That was so spectacular." Phoebe is hugging her, likewise Maggie.

She turns and sees her father, tears in his eyes. A special look passes between them. It is a connection of the past: her mother. Joyce loved that song, and she had taught her as a little girl. They often sang it together as a duet at church. Suddenly, she understands that her mother must have sung it for him. She lowers her eyes, unwilling to let Phoebe see. Life is rough enough; she does not want friction between these two and with four children! That is a no-no.

As the children gather around, telling her she sounds great, she nods and thanks them.

"Well, honey, anytime you want to come to the Bronx to stay, you are very welcome to do so. St. Barnabas Church will love you. Such a voice should not be wasted. My Verne, you play, and she sings. What a beautiful combination. You could have a father-daughter duo. Yes, yes, that would be perfect. Goodness, and one day, you may end up at Carnegie Hall," Maggie enthused.

Madison walks off, and her father stops her and hugs her. "You have a beautiful voice. I never knew you sang. Thousands should hear you sing. A talent like that should be enjoyed," he said.

"I did not know you played," she said with a smile.

"We have a way to go, Madison. We have to learn about each other. We may have more in common than we realize, except for the obvious."

"True," she nods and walks slowly to her room as her companion hails her. Jan takes her hand, and they move off to Maddi's room. She decides to tell Jan a story. "One day, a man named Jesus was traveling in Judea, and you know the children's mothers thought it was a good idea to take them to see Jesus so He could bless them. But Jesus's very best friends told the mothers to go away and not bother Him. And Jesus said to His friends, 'Oh, no, let the children come. They are very precious. Everyone should accept God's Word as the children do.' So He put His hands on them and blessed them. Isn't that neat?"

Jan nods as if she understands every word. Madison smiles and kisses her cheek. Who knows when understanding starts anyway, she muses. "Horsy," said Jan. "Horsy, horsy." She pulls at Maddi. "Maddi horsy."

Maddi understands finally. She is saying horsey. That is her favorite game, but she usually plays with her father. She puts her on the bed and turns her back. Jan immediately climbs up. She prances around for a while with Jan laughing and calling horsy. Madison walks to the backyard, coaching Jan. "Dada is horsey."

Madison walks to her father, stating Jan wants big horsey. Her father takes her and hoists her on his shoulder. Jan is laughing, so trusting, loving her new position. Madison looks at her and sees how innocent and carefree things are for her.

Her thoughts drifted to her mother's journal or book. What else would she find in there? She feels conflicted about whether to continue reading now or wait for another time. Phoebe's parents' arrival pushed all that into the background. Will reading it cause more heartache? Is she putting off the inevitable?

With this feeling of goodwill and camaraderie, it may be better to read it now. She repeats to herself repeatedly, the right atmosphere, the right atmosphere. She enters her room, pulls the book from the nightstand, and begins to read. Hurt by Verne's mother's words, she knew she was on her own. She was pregnant, but only she knew that. It was her secret. She did not confide in anyone. She missed Verne terribly, but one thing was sure: she would keep this baby. This baby was special. She would continue to audition for dance roles but would only go for short-term off-Broadway shows or temporary positions. Her waist would not stay small for much longer. She would teach more dance classes until it was obvious.

At three months, she told Carol and swore her to secrecy. She would tell her parents when she was ready. She longed for Verne so much, and the thought of him coming back kept her sane. She had a beautiful dream that he came home. They were dancing in the park, a man and a woman alone. There were stars that night, and the velvety voice of Gladys Knight's "Best Thing That Ever Happened to Me" was vivid and real. She could feel the strong arms around her.

Later in his apartment, she told him about their baby. He was ecstatic. He lifted her up and spun her around. He yelled, "I am going to be a father," and then he sang to her Paul Anka's song "Having My Baby." It was so real, and she knew then nothing could prevent them from having their baby. "Having my baby—what a lovely way of saying how much you love me. You are having my baby." She found the record and recorded it on cassette, inserting her voice. Paul Anka would not know, she reasoned, and he would forgive a pregnant woman whose love was at war.

Madison closes her eyes, overcome with emotions. Her mother loved her dad. What she held in her heart was immovable. It explained so much. She remembered one occasion her mother was wearing a pair of white pants with a black blouse and how gorgeous she looked. A group of men were admiring her. She told her mom, who just brushed it off. One of them tried to get her number, and she declined. The man was handsome. She quizzed her mother, who told her he was not her type. She was born to wear spandex. She had a killer figure. That was when she coined NVSE (Not Verne's Standard of Excellence). No one could replace Verne.

She explained she would always love him. Their separation was hardship but not founded on bitterness. They separated at the height of their love. No hostility, no acrimony, so no disillusionment, just joy of loving each other; hence her love was whole and clean. There was no hate. It is for that reason Rita Coolidge's "I'd Rather Leave While I'm in Love" resonated with her. Yes, her mother agreed it was better to leave while you were in love.

"Madison, darling, you are crying," the calm voice of Percy said. Her door is open, so he just walks in. He sits on the bed and holds her. "I know. It is your mother, right?"

She nods without answering. He continues to hold her, not talking but rocking her gently. "My mother said I am a gift from God, but where is she? Why isn't she here with me? I believe we keep our gifts, cherish them. I do not understand. It is so hard to see a loving God right now."

"We do not know everything. We have to live by faith. We have to believe God does not make mistakes. Hear me out. We are here for a while on this earth. She was here for as long as she was supposed to, to give you life. Your birth was her gift to the world, so you can soar and excel. Your voice, Madison, is not an accident. A voice like yours will thrill thousands. Look at the beautiful, sensitive young woman she reared. She did what she was put here to do. You are her greatest accomplishment. We or you want her here longer to be with us because it is hard to be separated from whom we love, but hold her in your heart, and she will never go." He touched her cheek and kissed the top of her head.

She desperately wants to believe everything Percy just said and hopes in time she embraces that her mother finished her race. Time will tell.

The high energy of the household would last throughout Grandma and Grandpa Thornton's visit. Sunday dinner is big and boisterous, comprised of shrimp, white crabs, and sausage combo, plus steak and oven-fried chicken with red potato wedges. Phoebe is now back in her familiar role as mom. Both she and Maggie work well together. The smoked sausages mixed with shrimp and crab make a pleasing aroma for the palate.

Madison could not wait to eat. She loves crab with smoked sausages. To her, the Creole delight is always welcome. She makes the lemonade with a twist of pineapple and tonic water. Jan seems to love crab meat as much as Madison, and she sicced her on her dad. Madison wants to enjoy the crab. She believes that crab meat is not saturated with fat, so she has her fill. "Why aren't you talking, Maddi?" asked Daniel. "You are very quiet today."

"I usually am when eating crabs."

"Why?"

"I need to concentrate on them. I can monitor the flow and make sure I get the last one," Maddi said.

Everyone laughs at the outrageous statement. Maddi shrugs and continues eating a claw with the pincers. The juice, slightly salty, is flavored with hot pepper, just as Maddi likes it. They can talk while she eats. Well, this is the only pot from which she will eat today. They are welcome to the steak and chicken. There is enough protein in this pot for her to be satisfied: corn, eggs, shrimp, carrots, and crabs, of course.

Life returns to normal as Grandma and Grandpa head home Monday morning. Things are back to normal, a sedate pace. Maddi goes through her clothes. Her assistant is more a hindrance rather than a help. Jan tries on Maddi's blouses and shorts. She puts the brassieres on her head and one arm through the strap. Each time Maddi places the clothes in the drawer, Jan takes them out. She stops briefly and twirls Jan around and drops her on the bed. Jan is laughing. "Jan, you know I love you, yes?"

Jan nods.

"But I will never get finished with you here, so do not help me anymore. Go find your parents and give them something to do. Just make a mess then run away to me, but take your time, okay?" said Maddi.

Jan nods, and Maddi carries her to the kitchen and urges her to go to her parents sitting at the table. "What happened? The duo has a falling out?" asked Phoebe.

"Oh, no, this half of the duo believes the other half has helped enough. One half puts in, the other takes out. See, no worries. She is a very good helper. Come back later, Jan," said Maddi.

Her parents laugh.

Maddi refolds the clothes but notices some of the tops are crushed, so she gets the iron and lightly presses these.

After an hour, she picks up her mother's journal and begins to read. She believes she is in better control of her emotions as she remembers Grandpa Percy's words. She reads again the pages where she describes her dream. This time, she looks through the box she'd grabbed before she'd left Canarsie. She finds the cassette marked Paul Anka. She opens the boom box that was a tri-purpose radio, cassette, and disc. She decides to listen closely to the words. Although she knows of it, she is not familiar with the words. She listens to the duet and understands why her mother said she changed it. She sang the part of Odia Coates.

It is such a beautiful sentiment, the nicest thing a man can tell a woman. There is love, devotion, appreciation, gratitude, warmth, and understanding, yet men walk away from their children too often. Maddi really understands for the first time the impact of her mother's decision. It is a choice. That line in the song resonates with her: "Didn't have to do it…could've swept it from your life, but you wouldn't do it…and you're having my baby." That is so powerful, she thinks as the words reverberate in her head. Every man who fathers a child should know this song and give it to his wife, fiancée, or girlfriend. There is risk to her health as well as the child. She knows the textbook version of preparation, but even that is enormous.

She wipes the remaining tears from her cheeks. She has to do better. She has become a big baby since her mom died. Lying on her back, she knows she must talk with her grandparents in Brooklyn. She will go tomorrow after the children leave for camp. Papa Verne will drop them off and then go to the hardware store and automotive store and then his shop. That way, he will not know of her plans and insist on taking her. She will tell Phoebe before she leaves.

Chapter 7

On Tuesday, as planned, she tells Phoebe of her plans to go visit her grandparents. She boards Metro-North train and heads toward Brooklyn. She takes the number 5 to Union Square and transfers to the L. She likes the trains. They move fast, and there is less traffic. However, today is different; there is train traffic. There is a sick passenger. Maddi sighs. She knows if she is lucky, it will take two hours or so. She will get to Canarsie later than expected.

She takes out her crossword so she can pass the time away. She becomes engrossed in it, and an hour and a half later, the trains start to move. Maddi is relieved, but it is almost midday, and she needs a bus to get to Avenue M and East Eighty-Seventh Street. She is not a fan of noontime sun.

Fifteen minutes later, she is on the B6 bus heading to her grandparents. With luck, the pious pair will be home. She will wait if necessary because she still has her key.

As she draws near her destination, she notices the car is missing and believes no one is home. She opens the door and hears her grandmother call out. Madison answers her. As she advances in the living room, her grandparents come from the kitchen. After the usual pleasantries, Madison explains she needs to ask a couple of questions, which she needs honest answers for. They agree to be honest with her. "Did my father, Verne

Moodie, come to visit my mother in 1991? How many times did he visit here?"

"Now look here, Madison, that was a long time ago. Mistakes were made, and we are very sorry about it. It was a mistake."

"Yes, but how many times did he come here? I was already born, so I basically have the same look I had as a child. I am asking you again: how many times did Verne Moodie come here looking for my mother?" she insisted.

"Okay, he came twice. He looked strange and seemed demanding. We did not know who he was and thought it better not to give him any information about Joyce."

"So he never spoke of the relationship with Mom? He never said it was urgent. Okay, so did he write to her?"

"Look, that is water under the bridge. We did not like the looks of him. He could have been dangerous. He did mention he was a vet. Those people sometimes suffer from shell shock and PTSD. We were protecting both of you. Do you think of that?"

"Yes, I have, but the question is did he write to her, and what became of the letters?" asked Madison. Her temper is fast rising, and she is getting impatient. "Well! Answer me. Where are the flipping letters?"

"Do not raise your voice at us. You are a child," said her grandfather.

"Hold that thought," Madison said, "the child part as it will give me reason if not the excuse I need. Where are the letters my father wrote? What did you do with them? Please answer me before the child starts to react."

"If you are going to continue in that tone, then the conversation is over. I think you better leave and come back when you are calmer and more respectful."

"Is that your answer too, Grandma? You are not saying anything. Where are the letters? Why in heaven's name did you never tell my mother? You think you are right to do what you did. How do you justify hurting your own flesh and blood? Were you never in love, Grandma? That was cold and callous. You took my father away from me," she said.

"Please leave, Madison. We haven't any more answers," her grandfather said.

"Wrong answer!" said Madison, and she picks up the crystal vase and aims it at the curio cabinet, where her grandmother's pride and joy are housed.

As she releases the vase, it goes sideways as she is grabbed from behind. "No, pumpkin, no!" her father said.

"Where the hell did you come from? I have unfinished business with the pious pair. I need an explanation. Where are the letters?" All this time she is struggling to get free, but his arms are steel.

"We did not mean to hurt you or your mother, Madison. Mistakes were made, I admit, but it was with good intentions," said her grandmother.

"Likewise, the road to hell is paved with good intentions!" said Madison.

"Leave before we call the police. You breaking things will not look good for you when they come.

"Why are you not answering?" said Verne. "What happened to the letters? Go ahead and call the police. I feel like throttling you myself, so please just answer. I am a vet. They will understand." He starts toward them, releasing Madison from the viselike grip.

Her grandparents move backward as Verne advances. They are clearly frightened. "We destroyed them. We did not mean any harm. We did what we thought was best for them. Once we realized too much time had elapsed, we thought that Joyce would have married, and Madison would have a father."

Madison started to cry. "You played judge, jury, and executioner and sentenced me to be raised in a single-family home when it was unnecessary. You Christians could not forgive your own daughter for being pregnant out of wedlock. You never loved me as Aunt Carol's children, and that is okay, but you had no right to deprive me of my father. That Baptist church you go to doesn't preach forgiveness? I see why Jesus had a problem with the religious people. They were the ones always in the temple. That's why my mother stopped going to that church. You set of hypocrites. But I hope you can find your conscience, though buried so deep in pride and self-righteousness," said Madison.

"Mr. and Mrs. Brooke, you did us a disservice. You judged me, and you are not God and failed to love your daughter and granddaughter. Everyone knows the connection between me and my daughter. We look so much alike. You did not even tell me I have a child. You mean Madison is not deserving of a father? What if Joyce had not run into my army buddy? I would not know I have a daughter.

"Do you know what you have done? Do you? As the years go by, why didn't you tell Joyce about me? You, by your malice, told everyone I am a deadbeat dad, that I refuse to know and care and support her. However, I leave you to your conscience because the conversation is not over. Your selfishness hurt Madison badly," Verne said. Verne shepherds his daughter through the living room and outside.

"Where did you come from?" asked Madison. "I did not need rescuing."

"Of course not," he said. "I am the guy that likes to butt in if his kid is in trouble or about to get in trouble. I called home, and Phoebe said you went to visit your grandparents. I got my van and just turned toward Brooklyn. I am happy I came. Why did you?"

"Their reaction when they saw you last week and the 'Oh my, what have we done?' or something like that. I am sorry I did not believe you that you came looking for Mom and did write to her."

"It's okay, Madison. I know it is a difficult situation. People made decisions for us long ago without thinking about the consequences. We just have to try to deal with it and not let it color your life, future, and relationships. There are always mean people. We learn to forgive and forget and move on. If we don't, we give them power over us, and they continue to hurt us and dictate our actions. Learn from it. I am not going to pretend it is easy because it is not, but work at it, but do not let it consume you," he said. Seeing the sadness on her face, Verne pulls off the road. "Come here!" He pulls her into his arms.

She reluctantly lets him draw her into his arms. He kisses the top of her head. "It will get better. Hang in there. I am not going anywhere. You will never walk alone. We can get through this. One by one, we will put these ghosts to rest. With every obstacle we overcome, we are stronger."

"You did love my mother?" she asked.

"I loved Joyce. She is a special person. I have no regrets meeting her or loving her. She loved me when I was unlovable, and I was. She coaxed goodness out of me and taught me not to hide from my emotions. That is priceless, and many have benefitted from that."

"I have to know. When you came to look for her, what was your intention?" she asked.

"I came because I wanted to marry Joyce. That thought alone kept me while I was in Iraq. She was my beacon of life and hope."

"So if my grandparents had not interfered, blocking the reunion with my mother, we would not be having this conversation. What if fate was kinder, or my grandparents—what would my life be?"

"Madison, the what-ifs are futile questions when the outcomes are known. That is one road you don't want to travel. It is only torture and torment. I cannot dwell on them. It would be as if I would have to negate my present life. Painful as it is, we must move forward. Yes, I regret what happened, but I cannot dwell on that. My vows are sacred to me and I would no more break with your mother than I would with Phoebe. In time, the hurt and pain will lessen. I felt like you did once. The biggest remedy is time coupled with love and patience. It will get better," he said.

She nods and pulls away from him. He is a great guy, like her mom said, but what would he do if he finds out his mother knew about Madison? She regrets not telling him last week when she read it. Now it is a dilemma. She decides to ask about his parents, the great Harold and Edith Moodie. His father is a Navy veteran who studied civil engineering, a tall and distinguished-looking gentleman who does not look his seventy-three years.

His mother is of average height, nicely covered with salt-and-pepper hair. The two make a stately couple; however, his mother tends to be snobbish. But they have been married for forty-seven years. They are dedicated to each other and have strong religious backgrounds. Grandfather Moodie was a clergyman who preached for over thirty-five years. He died some fifteen years ago, and his wife, Grandma Lilieth, died five years ago. She would have loved them, and he is sure they would have loved her. They were very nice, kind, and giving. The cleft in the chin was his legacy to them. His parents live on the other side of Mount Vernon.

"Do you ever go there? I mean, since they are snowbirds," Madison asked.

"Indeed, I do, but Mrs. Thomas goes to dust and air the place once per week. Her husband maintains the grounds."

"How big are the grounds?"

"I believe almost half an acre. There are a few trees—oak, etc.—and fruit trees: pears, apples, and peaches. Plus, there is a flower garden. Mr. Thomas does a great job. Do you want to have a look before we go home?" he asked.

Madison nods, then said, "Yes, that is a great idea. I am looking forward to it."

They arrive home after two. Phoebe opens the door with concern on her face. Her eyes dart from father to daughter, and Madison mumbles everything is fine. Madison hollers for Jan without answer. "You know she was fussy this morning, so unlike her. She kept looking in the rooms, as if looking for something or somebody. Since I was present and she kept looking, I guess it wasn't me. She has new friends now. I feel so rejected. Anyway, she is sleeping peacefully," said Phoebe.

Madison realizes Phoebe's rambling is directed at her, but she refuses to take the bait. She goes to find Jan and misses the look between the couple. She kisses Jan, and she smiles in her sleep. Madison knows Jan is her Achilles' heel, and if she were to leave, here—.

She cuts her thoughts short. That is something she does not have to think of right now. Tomorrow is soon enough. She smiles to herself. She examines the information about her paternal grandparents, although she asked her father whom he resembled because there are pictures of his children but not his parents or siblings. He laughed and said it was a secret, and she should wait and see. I will see because they are coming next Wednesday, and she will surprise the stately couple. This time, she will not tell anyone. She wants to see the ogre, aka the snob. Well, she is on a roll, so why stop now? Her maternal grandparents must be happy her father showed up out of the blue, literally a real hero in real life. He is showing himself as wonderful and dependable.

Madison is determined to keep her smile in place for the rest of the week and the next. She admits it is a little challenging, but it is something that she must do. She wants to bare the ogre in her lair. Wednesday cannot come fast enough. She wants to see her face when she confronts her and how much she looks like the commander without the facial hair.

Wednesday dawns brightly. The sky is a rich azure, with fluffy clouds and not hot or humid. It is a perfect day. She selects a cream-colored dress with orange and blue flowers. It is a pretty summer dress with spaghetti straps. For good measure, she puts on a pair of black shorts; after all, she is going to bike to Grandma's house.

Once the children leave for camp, she gets ready. She has to give Jan the slip so she does not fuss or want to accompany her. Nothing is to ruin her plans. Her plan is to tell Phoebe she is going for a ride before it gets too hot. She wants to test her endurance. She will leave after her father leaves for the garage. Fortune smiles as Jan sleeps. Once her dad leaves, she tells Phoebe of her plan, gets her helmet, tote, mask, sunglasses, water bottle, and paper towels.

She reaches the senior Moodies and rides up the driveway, parks the bike, and rings the doorbell. It seems like forever, but it is only seconds before the door opens. A slender lady greets her and asks how she can help. Madison answers from behind sunglasses, "Joyce Brookes." She is hoping Verne told her of her mother's death and, if she remembers, will be frightened.

The lady motions her in, closes the door, and walks rapidly away. Alone, Madison looks around. She quickly puts the latex mask on, being quite efficient at this, so by the time Mrs. Moodie asks her to join her in the sunroom, it is safely in place.

Madison gasps as she sees Mrs. Moodie and hopes she does not hear the swift intake of breath. Mrs. Moodie asks how she can be of help, if she is selling cookies. Madison improvises that they are starting a small newspaper and she is interviewing prominent residents. Her face loses the austere look. Mrs. Moodie states her husband is tinkering in the back garden and is not immediately available. She asks what she thinks are important questions, then asks about her children. She tells her she knows of her son, the vet, Commander Moodie. Maternal pride oozes from her lips. She asks about the recent addition to his family. She seems uncomfortable, and Madison pushes her about when they knew of this child, the child's mother, and if she has ever met her.

Mrs. Moodie says, "I have never met the mother and will meet the child on Friday."

"The child? Isn't that your granddaughter?" asked Madison.

"Of course, she is. I just have not met her yet. We were away and just returned. We will see her on Friday," she added.

"Oh, you seem hesitant. I am thinking grandparents always welcome grandchildren. Maybe you have a personal reason for your hesitancy," said Madison silkily.

"I don't appreciate the tone or your insinuations. I think this interview is over. Thank you, and have a good day."

"Yes, I will leave, but before I do, I want to tell you something and show you something. You prevaricate about knowing your granddaughter's mother. You met. As a matter of record, she came to see you when she was pregnant, didn't she? You disparaged her. She wanted to hook Verne. You would wait for the nine months as proof she was pregnant to see if the baby was Verne's. How am I doing so far?"

"She did not come from your social circle, so the first time you met her, Verne's high school date came to dinner too just so she would see she did not belong. Oh, yes, and should the baby be his, you would take him, raise him, and Joyce would be monetarily compensated. And lest I forget, you were to notify her when Verne's body came back from Iraq."

Mrs. Moodie's face turns from beet to orange to onion, and she starts to breathe shallowly, holding her chest. "Who are you? Where did you come from? Where did you get your information from? Get out! Get out! Harold. Harold," she called.

"I am going, but take a look at this."

Madison pulls the latex mask from her face, and Mrs. Moodie reaches for the back of the chair for balance. "Oh God. Oh Savior. You look, you look—"

"Yes, I look like Verne. Uncanny, isn't it? I am Joyce's daughter. See, she loved my dad and would not sell her baby, so I save you a trip. You do not have to come and see me Friday. Then you get to tell your son that you knew my mother was pregnant, that you offered to buy the baby, and all these years kept quiet. Have a nice day, Mrs. Moodie…I mean, Grandmother. Can I call you that?"

Madison walks out and runs into Lt. Harold Moodie. His look shows shock, bewilderment, and fright. "Who are you? Stop, please," he said.

"Go see to your wife. She needs you more than your need to know who I am. She may need the doctor," said Madison. She feels a tinge of conscience when she remembers Edith Moodie's pallor and her fright and quick gasps of breath. The lady who let her in looks at her, mouth gaping and eyes bulging.

Madison lets herself out. Let them deal with the chaos. Now she remembers why it is said misery likes company. She breaks her grandparents' crystal vase, narrowly missing the curio cabinet thanks to her father. This time, their son is not the hero. He is unaware of what just happened. She feels deflated; I guess that is what is called anticlimax. The high is not there.

Madison pedals along. She has no exact destination in mind. She will just ride until she is exhausted. She wonders if her grandparents will call Verne, and what will they tell him? What a mess.

Madison finds a grassy shady patch and sits. It is hot, but if she stays too long, it will get hotter, and her energy will sap. She is thankful for the shade. Invariably, introspection intrudes, something she does not want to deal with. She needs activity, so with extra pep, she jumps on her bike. She will walk downtown and visit the historic district. Maybe she will encounter some ghost or meet an out-of-towner. She is not in love with her thought as she is feeling guilty and can't help wondering if Mrs. Edith Moodie is all right.

Madison cannot escape her thoughts, so she decides to ride some more. She will go to the zoo instead. Halfway there, she encounters the minister of the Anglican church. He engages her in conversation. He asks how she is settling in and hopes she becomes a member of the church soon. He says more young people are needed in church. He hopes she will become active in the church as he hears she is a terrific singer. Madison laughs, telling him someone is teasing him. He says if she ever needs to talk, he is available, and he is cheap; there is no cost.

He continues that people do not know everything, understand most things, and sometimes make choices on limited knowledge and false claims. Mankind is accountable for their choices, but God's mercy and forgiveness go a long way to free us from guilt and shame of these choices.

She thanks him for his wisdom and assures him she will take him up on his offer one day. She abandons the zoo and enters the church, with its stained glass windows playing over the pew. The stone-cut walls make the inside cool, and Madison sits watching the play of light through the window. She dozes and is awakened by children. Oops! She has to get home. She calls the house, gets no answer, but leaves a message she will be home within the hour.

Madison starts home. Despite the heat, she is pushing it. She rounds the corner where the trees form a canopy, and an open-body truck swings too wide and catches her handlebar. Madison is thrown off her bike and sees her body flying through the air and cries, "Dad!" She hits the ground, and she sinks into oblivion.

Chapter 8

Verne's head is under the hood of the Ford he is working on. He hears Madison's voice call him. He answers and, without thinking, jerks upward and bangs his head on the hood. "Ouch! Darn it," he said, rubbing his head.

"Who are you answering?" said Gus, his army buddy. "Can't get Iraq out of you? War's over, my man."

"I tell you, I hear Madison's voice call me. I am not hearing things. It was clear: 'Dad.'"

"Okay, pal, whatever you say. You have been slacking off since your older daughter came, so I guess you want to take off again to rescue her. Oh, by the way, when am I going to be formally introduced to my honorary niece?" said Gus.

"When you start respecting your elders," said Verne with a smile. He was a day older than Gus.

"Wow! Older by a whole day."

"Yes, and don't forget it," Verne said.

Although he joked with Gus, a chill suddenly comes over him. He decides to call home. There is no answer, and he goes back to repair the truck, but is uneasy, so he decides to call home again. This time, he speaks with Phoebe. She said everything is all right, except Madison went for a ride and is not back. Phoebe denies being worried, rather concerned. That is enough for him, and he tells Gus he is pushing off for the day, but he should be on standby in case he needs him later.

One look at Phoebe tells him she is worried. He gets on his bike and sets off to look for her. He goes to the usual route along the road and along the trail. He is not sure she goes as far as the broken-down oak tree, but he goes beyond that anyway. There are tire tracks. He doesn't notice any skid marks or anything unusual. His heart is thumping so loud in his ears; he stops to shake his head.

He rides on and on before he realizes that he has been riding for an hour, so where could she be? He calls to no avail. Now he is sorry he didn't ask any of the bikers if they had seen her. The terrain in this area is rough, and he cannot believe she is beyond the hill above. He retraces his steps, calling intermittently. On one of his stops, he asks a young man if he saw her. He explains Madison looks exactly like him. The young man assures him he has not seen her.

Instinct tells him she did not run away, and she is in trouble and that he has to find her very soon. He rides toward the zoo, then decides against it and hopes she is headed home. He sees a pizza delivery boy and asks if he had seen Madison, always repeating, "She looks like me."

He realizes that is inadequate. He knows he cannot file a missing person's report as yet. He always thought the law was ridiculous and guesses maybe that's why there's an Amber Alert. He is conflicted about going to the police for an Amber Alert as she is just shy of eighteen years old. He cannot prove imminent danger, just gut. She is not going to thank me for drawing all that attention to her. What is his option? His gut tells him she is in danger.

There's only one course of action. He will round up his army buddies. He will call the Shadow Down, a group of navy men that does not exist. They get in places ordinary others can't. They move by stealth and are more silhouette than themselves. No one sees them, hence the name.

He rides with urgency back home. All the children are home and want to know where Madison is. He reluctantly informs them he did not find her but will go out again to look for her, but with his army buddies. He activates the signal and gives his coordinates.

Daniel comes back with flyers of Maddi, stating she is missing and asking people to call the number listed. His father congratulates him but tells him he cannot go out to hand them out or post them. One of his children missing is too many. Tomorrow, he can if he and his friends do not find her; they can use the flyers. He acknowledges Daniel's initiative and talent. He takes some of the flyers.

Soon his friends start arriving. They are dressed in black with vests and harnesses. He kisses his family goodbye. Jan is fussing and wants Maddi. He promises her he will bring her back. He tells her to send a kiss to Maddi, and it seems to help. The men ride away in the late glow of the evening sun. Each knows what he has to do. They each have a flyer with Madison's picture. He ignores the wows and whistles when they see her face. Inwardly, he smiles.

His heart is heavy with fear, mind burdened with dread. He leads the way, and the nine men follow closely. He is not convinced that no one has seen her. He runs into another delivery person and shows the flyer, and he says he believes he saw her about one o'clock. She was sitting under a tree near the church, drinking water. He calculates that is six hours ago. The group splits into three groups. One will go toward the zoo, the other toward the factories, and the other in the historic district. He goes toward the historic district. Gus and Dale accompany him.

After about fifteen minutes, he stops Sheriff, a mental health patient. He talks to him, then asks if he has seen Madison. He tells him yes, but the truck passed, and she is gone. He tries to get more information. Finally, he says she did not go in the truck. The way he shows his hand seems like something scattered.

Verne is excited. He urges Sheriff to tell him where he saw her and the truck. He insists at the corner with trees. He has to be satisfied with Sheriff's description and heads in that direction of the area where the foliage is thick in areas and tall trees that form a canopy. That area is about a mile long, and he and the others agree to spread out to cover more ground.

Verne is happy to be alone. He feels like crying; his grief is so profound but is too embarrassed to display such emotion. Alone, he lets the tears flow. He searches every thicket, every underbrush, every inch of the terrain. He must find her. Failure is not an option; the stakes are too high—Madison's life. Joyce entrusted her to him, and in a few short months, he has lost her. He hacks away with his machete. Finally, he gives in to the despair he is feeling.

He cries out to the God he's ignored and begs for the life of his daughter. Tears streaming down his cheeks, his cries are broken sobs. He cries for the love he lost, for Joyce for dying so young, for loving him enough to have his baby even against her parents' opposition, and knowing she would have to raise the baby alone. He cries as he was oblivious to his own child. He cries for the last time for his lost love. As he cries, he asks God to lead him to his daughter.

"Hear me, oh God," he pleads. "Do not take her life. Let me find Madison. I love her so. Do not hold my sin against her. Have mercy on me." And he sees the water bottle and the mangled bike. This energizes him, and he hacks with renewed purpose. He is a man driven, but he now has hope.

It is dark now, and the foliage is thick, and even with his flashlight, it is difficult with the uneven land. Verne keeps going, forgetting he must send a flare. He loosens his rope and ties it to a tree, the harness fastened securely around his waist. Flashlight swinging, he goes down the slope. Which way should he go? Then he sees this beam of light, and he follows the moving light. He does not grasp that he does not see an actual person; he just knows he has to follow the light. Eventually, it stops and hovers, and that is when he sees her. He is hysterical. He is laughing and crying. He sees his baby. "Yes! Yes! Thank You, God. You still answer prayers."

He makes his way gingerly toward Madison. A sapling was holding her limp body. Her face is pale in the light, her hair matted with blood. He touches her gently. She seems so fragile. He kisses her cheek. Leaves and twigs are embedded in her hair, and he belatedly feels for a pulse. She is alive. He unhooks the extra hook and fastens it to his. He is unsure if he can climb back up or seek lower ground.

While he is debating, the sapling that held Madison snaps in two. He clutches Madison, although she is safe. What if he halts his thoughts? He knows the harness will hold, and he needs to notify the others, but he is holding Madison as well as his harness. It seems simpler to edge his way down the slope. It is painstaking, but he does. He sends up a flare. He turns on his radio, advising his pals he found Madison.

As he awaits his friends, he cradles her in his arms. She opens her eyes briefly as she asks who he is. He replies he is her dad. She looks at him, lips about to smile, and closes her eyes. She does not wake again until she gets to Montefiore Hospital. The commander is bruised, scratched, dirty, hands bleeding with calloused hands, but is happy. God showed him favor. He has no complaints.

Two days later, Madison woke up. The doctors elected to let her sleep due to the head injury. She sustained a broken left arm, badly bruised ribs, and a two-inch gash at her hairline above her left eye. The unknown was if there was severe nerve damage. Verne did not leave the hospital despite pleas from doctors and nurses. Phoebe sent for her parents so they could stay with her and the children.

Verne was present when she woke up. She smiles and says hello. "Madison! You are awake. Oh, thank God," he said.

"Who is Madison?" she asked.

"You, baby. That is your name. I am Dad, your father."

"Me Madison? You are Dad. I don't remember. This is a hospital. What am I doing here?" she asked, getting anxious.

"Nurse! Nurse!" Then he pushes the call button. Hasty feet herald two nurses. "My daughter is awake," he said triumphantly.

"We will call Dr. Rowe. Welcome back, Madison. You came in two days ago. You had an accident," said Nurse Lee. "Don't you remember?"

But Madison gazed at her with a blank look. "I do not remember any accident. I remember Dad but nothing else."

The nurse smiles and tells her not to worry. Patients with head injuries sometimes forget. Her head begins to throb, and she puts her right hand to her head. "My head hurts. Dad, Dad," she said tearfully.

Instantly, he is with her and holding her. By then, the doctor walks in. "Madison, you are awake. How do you feel? Let me see," he said and asks Verne to leave.

Madison clings to him and starts to cry. The doctor frowns, wanting to know what is happening, why she is crying. Verne answers him. He tells the doctor she cannot remember the accident or her name. The doctor asks about her family, if she has siblings, their names, and her parents, if she has a pet, or if there is anything she remembers. With each question, she grips her father tighter and tighter. The doctor tells them not to worry. She will be all right and that sometimes, persons experience temporary memory loss and not to worry. He said he will give her medication for the pain. Madison loosens her grip somewhat. "Dad, where is my mother? I have sisters and brothers."

"Yes, there are four children. The youngest is twenty-one months. She is your favorite. Her name is Jan. Well, there is Daniel, the oldest boy, and the twins, Charles and Chelsea. Daniel is outgoing, incredibly talented with computers. Charles is a little shy, loves chess. And Chelsea is friendly, an avid chess player. And my Madison sings," he said, kissing her head.

"Whom do I resemble, you or Mom? I like hearing about my family, so Jan is my favorite. Well, who do I look like?" she asked.

"I will not tell. Do you know little girls adore their fathers? Can you tell? Jan adores me when you are not there. You are in college at NYU.

You will be eighteen in a couple of weeks. See, I have a brilliant daughter who is already a sophomore."

"I think I look like you. Your sound has that self-satisfied chuckle. I am sleepy, Dad. Are you going to be here when I wake up?"

"Yes. Nothing would take me from you," he said, kissing her brow.

Verne eases Madison to the center of the bed and settles himself more comfortably on the bed, her head resting on his shoulder. He is very happy. Madison clings to him, wanting him around. He cannot help wondering if this would have been the life if he had married Joyce. Madison loves him. Despite the circumstances, he is enjoying it. He knows she has amnesia, or else she would not be chummy with him.

He hears her soft, shy voice as she settles herself snugly on his shoulder. The doctor walks in, saying nothing about where he is. He knows half the nurses are intimidated by him. Anyway, he is good for her. He decides to give Dad the news about Madison. He smiles and looks at the chart. "Well, Mr. Moodie, it seems that Madison has retrograde amnesia. It's loss of memory before the accident. She has lost facts, not skills. This is usually short term and returns on its own. I am sure the bump on the head is the culprit. There seems not to be any major swelling. There was some bleeding but seems to have stopped, and we will monitor this a couple more days. A few more tests and we will determine if there is any nerve damage. Because of the headache and possibly dizziness, tomorrow we will test her gait," said Dr. Rowe.

"I know a little about amnesia. I am okay with that as long as it is not permanent. She was unconscious for a long time, and that two-inch gash is no joke. Thank you, doctor," he said.

He continues to hold Madison, still fearful for her life. He knows he is neglecting the other children, but after that sobbing and plea for her life down in the slopes, he just cannot leave her. He closes his eyes and prays for courage to leave her and do more than go home and change clothes. He promises to go home and speak with the children and give Phoebe time to visit. With this plan, he is content. He calls home, calls his parents, siblings, and his army buddies. He also calls her maternal grandparents as well.

The next day, he goes home and explains to his children what is happening. He explains about the amnesia. He omits to tell them she is not walking. He remembers the conversation with Madison and how she urged him to go look for the family, as she said Phoebe needed to see him as well as the children.

Tests show no nerve damage. There is no swelling at the base of the brain. However, Madison is lethargic, and her balance is off. Verne and Phoebe visit, and they hug. Madison naturally refers to her as mother. Phoebe is content for now to let it go. They chitchat mostly about the siblings. Madison briefly refers to her inability to walk even though tests reveal no reason why she shouldn't, but maybe the brain is not responding to the signal. The doctor is not worried about it yet.

Phoebe leaves with the promise of kissing Jan for Madison. Her father stays, being worried about her lethargy. He looks for the doctor but finds the nurse instead. He expresses his concern, especially since her balance is off, unable to sit up, tilting to the side and sliding down in the bed. The nurse comes in, observes, and agrees to call the doctor. Her paternal grandparents visit, but Madison does not respond to them. She is quiet and seems almost afraid of them. She feels hostile toward them, which makes no sense as she does not know them. Her father never said they met, so why this feeling? Her head begins to hurt, and she is happy when they leave. They appear as uncomfortable as she is.

The doctor comes and orders a CT scan of the brain with contrast. He is concerned about the lethargy and lack of balance. The test revealed a blood clot. Within minutes of the result, Verne signs the authorization for surgery. He calls Phoebe to update her and asks that she tell the others. He will stay.

Verne remains in the room and goes back to praying. He is the happiest he has been since he learned of Joyce's illness. The relationship with his daughter is everything he desires and more. He knows he is on borrowed time and walking on a tightrope, but he is a drowning man, willing to grasp at straws. He prays for the doctor and team and asks for his daughter's life once again. He cannot lose her.

Prayer over, he keeps his head on the bed. Part of his prayer is for solace, and he gets it. He falls asleep. In his dream, Madison is running with Jan in Central Park. Daniel and the twins are playing football. He is blessed and content.

He awakes and sees it is four o'clock. He goes to the nurse, and she states that surgery is over and she will be returning shortly to the room.

A week after her surgery, she still cannot walk. She has physical therapy daily, and her feet remain stubborn, refusing to move. Her routine is to have therapy. Her father helps her and holds her, but there is little improvement. She has feelings in her legs, but the transfer request to move is lost somewhere between the legs and the brain. Verne feels a compulsion to help his daughter. He is no medic, but he has heard stories of miracles happening where persons walk against the odds. He knows the body reacts to shock and stress and wonders if something shocks Madison, it would make her walk. God knows he enjoys the closeness, wants it to continue, and the human side interjects, What if the shock not only restores her gait but her memory as well, revealing they were only civil and not loving as they are now? Is he willing to risk that? It is a dilemma, but he has to give her the chance to recover. Love is free. Love is not selfish. He repeats these statements. His heart is breaking, but he has no choice but to do the right thing. He prays for the courage to do so. Things are never always clear-cut.

The next day, Verne tells her she is going to rehab as her surgery went well, and both wounds are healing well. Another week, and she is going home. After her therapy session, Verne tells her he is leaving and is not coming back for the day. She says okay until his words penetrate her consciousness. He turns and walks away, and she panics and calls to him to wait. He continues walking, and she bounds out of her chair, asking him to stay with her. Without thinking, she makes unsteady steps toward the retreating back of her father. "Dad!" is the plaintive cry.

He turns, and she is walking. Madison stops in surprise when she realizes she is walking. He holds out his hands, urging her to come to him. She starts to cry, stating she can't. "Yes, you can, baby. Come to me. You are doing great."

Still crying, she takes tentative, hesitant steps. With her father encouraging her, she walks to him. He picks her up and spins her around. "I knew you could do it, and you did. Yeah!"

The nurses run to see the commotion. They cheer her, congratulating her, saying maybe she does not need rehab now. She will have to be steady on her feet. Physical therapy and the doctor will make the decision. Verne walks her to the chair, afraid the excitement is too much as she is trembling. He is so happy. He kisses her brow. He tells her everyone will be happy she is walking.

Madison was discharged home, and her amnesia continued. Verne still carried the secret of their relationship. Things returned to normal as much as possible. Madison resumes her friendship with Jan. She spends her time with her baby sister. She has visitors daily from her father's army pals and Father Bernard, minister of the Anglican church she spoke with the day of her accident. He tries to get her to recall the conversation, but this proves futile. He prays and leaves.

That evening, her parents inform her that her friends Pam, Joan, and Phil want to visit. They said it is up to her. They already explained about the amnesia to them, but there's no pressure to see them. Madison agrees to see them. Her friends are lively and entertaining. Pam's eyes look like saucers upon seeing the father and his two daughters. "Geez, stars of wonder. What? Three people look so much alike. Wow! Oh my gosh. Don't you all frighten yourself, really?" said Pam.

The others laugh at Pam's statement. Joan and Madison are rolling their eyes.

"It's a good thing you all are handsome, good-looking people. Can you imagine if it were the opposite? Boy, that would be a whole lot of ugly bunched up in one place," said Pam.

With that statement, everyone started to laugh. The laughter continues for several minutes. Madison laughs long and loud. She has a feeling of déjà vu. Pam is definitely the entertainer! "Pam, you are outrageous."

"Well, I'm just saying. The first time I saw Mr. Verne here, I did a double take. He couldn't hide he is the papa, but to see another person with the same face is stupendous. Anyway, did you meet any dishy doctor up there? Any dishy doc can check my heart anytime. So come on, girl, everyone had horns and a fork. Well, you had PT. Who was it? What! He had two heads."

Madison laughs. "Yes, there is a child prodigy. He is twenty-one, in his fourth year, and specializing in cardiology—Dr. Ridge Carr, and then there is PT Bryan Aguilar. Sorry, I know very little about them. I'll keep you in mind when next I go for my checkup," she said.

"Mr. Verne, are you up for cooking?" Pam asked.

"No," he said. "Are you?"

"I am sorry, Mr. V. The pot, stove, saucepan, and spoon and I had a quarrel. We ended up in divorce court for irreconcilable differences. The utensils won, and we went our separate ways, but we are divorced but friendly. I don't bother them, and we are good. So how about that food?" said the delightful Pam.

By this, everyone is laughing. Madison sees the ease with which her friends relate to the family. She is comforted by this. Her dad good-naturedly gets the grill and grills hamburgers, hot dogs, and corn on the cob. The drinks flow freely, and everyone seems satisfied. Her friends leave, and the cleanup starts. There is a feeling of goodwill all around. Jan is in the thick of things, helping, picking things up.

That night, Madison lies in bed, thinking about her reaction to her father's parents when she was in the hospital. She finds her reaction strange. Does she know them? But how? She will have to ask her dad tomorrow.

Verne sighs and sits on the bed, awaiting Phoebe's return from the bathroom. He smiles as she emerges, her short satin pajamas showing off her thighs. He begins to talk. He says he feels like he is living on borrowed time. He is happy but worried. Madison is so into him that he is afraid to tell her things that could possibly bring her memory back. He needs her to love him but not by default. Yet he is reluctant to risk the camaraderie, but what if she remembers they were antagonistic prior to her memory loss? The what-ifs are killing him. In another week or so, it will be the Fourth of July, and the whole family will descend. She had a run-in with Jennifer, and her knack for tactlessness might create a colossal disaster. He has no intention of deceiving Madison, but he feels burdened. He then asks her to pray with him.

The next morning, he tells Phoebe he has made his decision. He will tell Madison everything. Guilt is heavy artillery. He cannot shoulder that. He will take Madison by his shop and then go to the park nearby, where they can talk. Phoebe calls him a traitor, leaving her to pacify Jan, who, he knows, is going to cry. He smiles, kisses her, and asks if she wants to offer a bribe. She throws a cushion at him.

Madison and her father left, and as predicted, Jan starts to cry. "Do we have to? I do not like when she cries," said Madison.

"We will be back shortly. We will stop at the shop briefly, and then we will go to the park to talk." As she turns to him, he says, "No. Can you see Jan sitting quietly and not in your lap demanding your attention? This is important, honey, something I have to do. I have to do so before the family comes for the holiday. The four siblings will be here with their children and my parents as well."

He pulls into the shop and introduces Madison to Gus. Gus has a quick smile, shakes Madison's hand, and his face is alight with merriment. "Nice to meet you in person. The last time I introduced myself, you ignored me, but I'm such a nice guy. I do not hold grudges. Ask your old man."

"Gus, shut up. He saw you when you were unconscious, so do not worry. He fancies himself a comedian."

Madison laughs. "Okay. For a minute there, I was wondering, but I see. So, you are a mechanic like Dad?"

"Nah," he said, "I am an enthusiast. Your dad is the real talent—fixes anything and everything. They miss him in the navy. Fix anything with an engine."

"You exaggerate, my friend. Madison, sit in the office for a while. I need to check something on this car."

About half an hour later, they are on their way to the park. He finds a bench under a tree. It is cool there, the sun not yet penetrating the leaves. He asks how she feels, if she is suffering any leftover effects from the day before. She assures him she is doing well, that she sleeps well at night. He inhales and begins his narrative. He wants to help in getting her memory back. She came to live with him in May. Her mother, Joyce Brookes, passed away in March. He was unaware of her birth until February. Years ago, they believed he died while removing land mines, but his vehicle hit a land mine, and he was thrown some thirty feet.

"No one told your mom otherwise, so she raised you by herself. While going through chemotherapy, she met Sergeant Torres, who told her I was alive. We made contact, and I saw her, and we made plans to tell you, but she passed before she could introduce us. Her dying wish was that I should care for you and for you to get to know me. You were furious as you believed I abandoned both of you. There was friction between us, but you got along with everyone in the household. We were polite strangers.

After a visit to Brooklyn one day, you found out I did tell the truth. I came back, looking for Joyce. Her parents never told her I came or wrote to her. Then one day, you said you were going for a ride. You did not come home."

His voice broke, and he struggled to speak. On the third attempt, he did. "I looked for you for hours. There was such a pain in my heart. I had never hurt like that since losing Joyce fifteen years ago." His arms held hers tightly. "I realized I had to get help. I ruled out the police as I wasn't sure if this qualified as an Amber Alert, and according to law, you must wait two days to file a missing person's report, so I called my navy buddies, the Shadow Down, and we combed the area.

"While I searched for you, I cried out to God to save you. I cried and pleaded for your life and asked Him to lead me to you. There was a light ahead of me, and although there was no form, I followed it. It led me to you and then disappeared. You were resting on a sapling. I strapped you to the harness, and the tree broke. I was laughing and crying and thanking God. You woke once and asked who I was, and I told you, 'Dad.' You half smiled and blacked out.

"That is why I could not leave while you were in the hospital. I was so afraid of losing you. I prayed that you would know how much I love you and would never abandon you."

His grip is much like a vise. Madison struggles to breathe. "Dad, Dad, I can't breathe," she said.

Slowly, he releases her. "I am sorry. Are you hurt?" his tone anxious.

She shakes her head. This is a lot to digest. "Oh, Dad, you are trembling. I am sorry. You must have been so terrified. Weren't you afraid to follow that light?"

"My fear was not finding you. I believed so strongly that God would answer that the moment I saw that light, I knew I had to follow. Most of all, Scripture says, 'Ask, and it shall be given.' I had nothing to lose and everything to gain. I thought afterwards that God didn't like to see a six-foot man cry."

"I am sorry I did not believe you. I am sorry for all the trouble and pain. You risked everything, Dad—your safety and family. You did not have to tell me all this."

"I had to! Besides, you are my family. I want to earn your love and trust, honestly. I love you, Madison Brookes-Moodie. I added my name to your birth certificate. You are mine, all mine."

She hugs him tightly. "Oh, so Phoebe is my stepmom. Ah, so when I was in the hospital, I just assumed that because she is your wife, she is my mother. Guess it was easier than explaining to people. Furthermore, it was none of their business anyway," she added.

"Do you know, the day of your accident, at about two or a little before two, I heard you call me, 'Dad.' I answered and bumped my head on the hood of the car I was fixing. Gus thought I was trying to go home early. I called home, but I was restless and just left shortly afterwards."

"Dad, have I met your parents? When I saw them in the hospital, I was afraid of them. I was uneasy."

"No. They were coming to visit on Thursday. They came in from Florida the Wednesday before. I took you to the house once. In a week or so, it will be July 4, and the whole family will be there. All four siblings will meet. There is James and his son Allan, Amina, her husband Shane, and children Conrad, Johnathan, plus Jennifer and Will Taylor and their two children, Caleb and Vanessa. Don't worry if you do not remember it all. Eventually, you will know them all. You already met Jennifer, and you had words. Jennifer is the tactless one in the family, but you handled it and would not tell me the details. Suffice it to say, Jen's nose was out of joint," he said with a laugh.

"When is my birthday? I do not even remember that."

"August 18, 1991. You can choose what you want to do for your birthday later. I like your friends, especially Pam. She is a riot."

"Really now. I am surprised. You like Phil too? He is afraid of you, and I don't know how I know that," she said.

"See what I say? I am beginning to like Phil. Smart guy!"

"Dad, you are six feet and muscular. Why wouldn't he be afraid of you? You keep eyeing him. Your eyes give the third degree, Dad. The nurses were afraid of you, the doctors, and the physical therapist. I'm not intimidated. You are on my side. Are you one of these mother-hen dads? You watch and hover!"

"My beautiful daughter, do you have somewhere to go? Wait and see. Just wait and see."

"You are not any different from Mom. I was to go out with friends when I was fourteen. She dropped me off. Later, we were walking towards McDonald's. There was Mom following. I was so embarrassed. Luckily, the others did not see her. At home, I asked her why she was following me, that I thought she trusted me. She trusted me, but I was all she had. 'Oh dear! And you know, I thought I was being discreet,' she said.

"'No, Mom, you are busted.' I just laughed."

Her father is looking at her in amazement with a broad smile. "Maddi!" he said.

"Oh, Dad, I had a memory. Did you notice? Did you notice? My head! I have a headache."

"Take it easy, honey. Do not get excited. Breathe."

He eases her backward so her head is resting across his chest. He gently massages her forehead and temple. "We will go soon. I wish I had my water bottle with me or saw one of those guys selling water," he said.

After about fifteen or twenty minutes, he asks her about her headache. She's on the verge of sleep but answers, "Better."

He slowly sits her up, and a minute later, gets up and bends toward her. She knows instinctively what he has in mind. "Oh no, Dad! You are not lifting me up. We walk."

"All right, but can I at least hold you so you don't stumble?"

"Can I stop you?"

"No."

"Didn't think so. Okay, Dad, let's go."

"Have you been having memory episodes with the same results?"

"Snippets, Dad, but with just a tinge. It is the first time I have such a complete memory of anything. Most of the time, it's like an awareness, like with Pam. I know she is the comedian in the group, and she will always entertain you, but never this distinct or the headache."

"We will call the doctor when we get home, and you can get in bed, and your babysitter Jan can stay with you. I notice she seldom leaves your side since you have been home. I believe she is afraid she will not see you."

The drive home is without incident. Her father's eyes never leave her for long. She cautions him to keep his eyes on the road. They reach a compromise. They talk all the way home. She persuades him to take her home rather than to the ER. Against his better judgment, he agrees; after all, her checkup/post-op was only five days ago.

Phoebe opens the door as they arrive. Face anxious, eyes questioning, she looks at one then the other. Madison greets her with, "Hi, Mom," and hugs her.

Jan is a closer second and gets out, "Maddi."

As Madison is about to pick her up, her father swoops in with, "Oh no, you don't." He picks Jan up and kisses her.

She dimples at him, momentarily distracted.

"What is the matter?" Phoebe asks. "I'm fine, Mom. It is your husband who is not fine."

Phoebe's lips twitch. "Will someone enlighten me, hmm?"

"Your daughter has a headache and does not want to go to the ER, so she agrees to come home and go to bed with a sitter. Now I decide she will have a second one. I do not want her picking up Jan until I am satisfied about that headache."

"Okay, Hover Dad. I am going, but you said Jan can be with me. And who is the next sitter?"

The look on her dad's face said everything. "I guess that he is sitter number two." She is tired and not as strong as she thinks she is.

As she settles down to sleep, the anguish on his face as he recounted how he searched for her comes back to her vividly. Tears fill her eyes, and the defiance slips from her, and she turns and faces him. She sits up in the bed, and he meets her halfway. "I love you, Dad," and he enfolds her in his arms, and Phoebe captures the moment—the reconciliation!

There is a flurry of activities for July 4. Phoebe and Verne are in charge, and they do a good job. Madison is the official babysitter, although she is unsure of who is watching whom. Jan does not let Madison out of her sight. She now sleeps with Madison, abandoning her crib. Madison does not mind now; she is accustomed to having her toe in her mouth or blocking her nose. It makes it easier for the parents to come in and kiss both children goodnight.

Most nights she is in bed with Jan to ensure she goes to bed at eight o'clock. Sometimes, Madison plays chess or Scrabble with the other children. Daniel seems to grow daily. He is well past Madison's height. It is not surprising, considering his lineage. One evening, Madison, curious about the tote by the bed, pulls it out. She pulls out her mother's journal. She reads with new eyes. The words are unfamiliar to her.

As she flips through, she notices a marker. She reads that her paternal grandmother knows of the pregnancy. So why doesn't she know them? Why didn't her mother contact her? She wonders if this is the reason for her uneasiness and veiled hostility. Her dad said they never met. She reads about her mother's dream where her father sings Paul Anka's song "(You're) Having My Baby." She chokes up again unknowingly. She plays the cassette and is amazed at the lyrics. With tear-filled eyes, she falls asleep.

The next day, as Phoebe cleans and engages in the rest of the household in that pursuit, Madison hears her humming a song. Surely it isn't! Her ears pick up the strain of "Having My Baby." She inches closer and is outside her parents' room when Phoebe calls to her. She walks in. Madison confesses she likes the song, and Phoebe asks her why. She tells her it is one of the best gifts a man could give to a woman. It is romantic, tender, and touching. Phoebe laughs and tells her, "Well said."

She tells Madison that Verne bought that when he found out she was pregnant with Daniel. Madison feels her face stiffen and closes her eyes. She prays nothing betrays her. I am going to be sick.

From a distance, she hears Phoebe ask if she is okay. She forces a grin and assures her she is. Madison leaves. What the hell is this? The same song! And he buys the record for Phoebe. Coincidence?

She feels weak, as if she is punched in the gut. She cannot think. She refuses to think, and she is not going to cry. With that determination, she throws herself into the preparation.

Independence Day dawns bright and crisp. Breakfast is a leisurely affair. Maggie and Percy Thornton are unsure if they will attend, but the rescue team and Verne's family will be there, and possibly Dr. Ridge Carr, Phoebe and Madison's secret guest. He is scheduled to work but is trying to get a switch, so it's maybe.

The different families come at different times. Amina and Shane arrive with their three children midmorning. Both are likeable, as are their children. Jean and Jan are months apart. Conrad and Johnathan are closer to Chelsea and Charles' age. They start playing early, and Jan and Jean join in. James and his son Allan James Jr. arrive next, with Jennifer being the last to arrive. James and his son are handsome, and the elder has conceit written all over his face. Not as handsome as my dad, Madison decides.

To take the pressure off, Madison has no expectations. She likes Vanessa and Caleb, Jennifer's children. As close in age and college students, they get along well. She talks freely about her amnesia as she rationalizes she did not buy it or ask for it. The plus, she tells them everything is new, and she will retain it better. They talk about summer jobs and internships. She is introduced to the rescue team and promptly forgets their names, except Uncle Gus and Vaughn.

She makes the effort to be civil and extra polite to her dad's parents. She sees them eyeing her covertly. She is tempted to ask them if they met but resists the urge. They respond in a civil manner, but the smile does not reach their eyes. Auntie Mina is gregarious and fun, likewise Uncle James. Uncle Will gives her a big hug, teasing her he didn't believe she could possibly have lost more weight. They met Memorial Day. Madison laughs. Her hair, about an inch long, frames her face attractively.

Madison is happy and tired. At eight, her father banishes her to bed, and she leaves with Jan. She is out like a candle in a gale. Her sleep is deep and dreamless. Jan's feet do not disturb her.

Chapter 9

Two weeks after the family gathering, Madison has a date with Ridge. She dares not agree to meet him anywhere else but home. Her father is a menace. She secretly believes his first name should have been Dennis. Even though Phoebe gives her permission, it takes some time convincing him about the date. He offers to bring her to the restaurant and take her back home. The man is out of control! She is going out with a doctor. If she panics, she will resign herself to spinsterhood. She appeals to Mom. She hears his belligerent tones that Ridge should find someone his own age, coming from the same man who was seven years her mother's senior. In the end, the compromise: he visits her at home.

The evening is uneventful, except Jan wants Maddi. They sit in the back by the arbor with drinks and finger food he brought. The food is tasty and flavorful. Ridge is a pleasant companion, and they talk and laugh. He likes comedy, jogs three days a week, and likes to dance. He is the third of five children. His father is a doctor, a neurologist, and two older brothers are doctors as well, an ophthalmologist and an internist. The two girls, Wanda and Jackie, want to be dentists. They are still in high school.

Madison is impressed. They are a brilliant family. She likes their easy conversation. He wants to visit again. He is not bothered by her father's behavior. She was in an accident, and he is being protective. TBI is serious, and her memory has not returned. He smiles disarmingly. When she walks him to the door, he kisses her cheek. It is a pleasant surprise, and she smiles.

The next day, she decides to give her memory a poke. She calls Pam but does not get her. What if she gets back on a bike? Daniel can accompany her. She knows her father will object, especially if he is not there. She tries to be patient, but it is difficult because her dad is inflexible. She decides they will ride half a mile and return home.

They ride to the green gates without incident, but outside their home, her bike slips, and she falls into the grass. She tells Daniel she is okay, and he checks her shoulder, head, and limbs. Mockingly, she asks him if she will live. He answers in the affirmative.

Her memory remains blocked, and she only remembers bits and pieces, like her English class and her grades or her philosophy class. She talks to Uncle Fitz and Aunt Carol, but it is only small talk. She talks about her mother working at Downstate Hospital and that she was a dancer and had a beautiful voice and went to the Christian Life Center. Still, her memory remains dormant.

Leaving the bathroom and hurrying to get her phone, she stubs her toes and falls. It is a harder fall than the one outside. She is winded and does not get up immediately. Wow, she thinks, this is a hearty hit. She sits up, then climbs onto the bed. She falls asleep without Jan. She has a dream about her life.

Two days later, in the quiet of the arbor, her memory comes back. She remembers everything. It is just like the pages of a book. She is reading her history, and as current events burst in her mind, she stops. The visit! She is aghast at what she did. Now she knows why her paternal grandparents shy away from her—and worse, from their grandchildren.

She remembers the pallor on Edith's face after she leveled the accusation against her. She realizes the mistrust, animosity on her side, the disconnect between her and them, and lack of warmth, of love. She will not tell her parents, especially her father. It will cause a rift that nothing can bridge. Her father will be livid. She cannot let this happen. She must make it right for Daniel and the others. She will go and see them. The bitterness she experiences should not pass on. Pain and hurt can poison the soul. She thinks to herself that they may not like her, but children are innocent and usually get hurt. She will not tell her parents, and she will take a cab. She will leave a note in her room just in case.

She reaches early afternoon, and her features, so like her grandfather's and father's, still seem to surprise them. The greeting is stilted, and she accepts this. She explains she wants to have a frank conversation with them and comes on her own. Her father is unaware of her visit. She declines refreshment but accepts water.

Several deep breaths, and she jumps in before nerves assail her. She apologizes for the accusations of her last visit. She knows two wrongs will never make a right. She is sorry because if it becomes public, it is suffering, recrimination, continued animosity, and will lead to an acrimonious situation. She never took into account her grandmother might have been grieving at the time or that other women might have used that ploy before. She does not want her father to know what she found, that her mother had contacted them, as it may cause irreparable damage between him and them and throughout the family. She does not worry about herself, but the other four children need their grandparents. She is ready to end it. Since they did not tell him she came there, then it is up to them what they tell. In the end, the biblical injunction "train up a child in the way, etc." is true.

"My mother never touted revenge or malice but rather forgiveness. Hurt people hurt others, and just as you hurt us, I wanted to pay you back for lacking the compassion for a pregnant young woman, for not saying to her, 'My son isn't dead.'

"However, it is not for me to judge, so I ask you to forgive the diatribe that foreshadowed my injury and subsequent amnesia. The amnesia is over, and I did not tell my parents, but I felt compelled to see you and ask for forgiveness. Thank you for listening, and I hope one day we can bridge the divide because, after all, we are family."

As Madison gets up, Edith reaches out and touches her hands and thanks her for her generosity. "I am so sorry, Madison. You are right about everything. Your mom must have been a phenomenal woman. She raised you right, and I am happy to have you as a granddaughter. I hope you can forgive me."

She crushes Madison to her, and Harold comes forward and hugs her. "Welcome to the family, Madison. You are indeed generous and from good stock. We are happy you are our granddaughter. If you looked any more like Verne, we would need a sign around each of your necks." He guffaws at his own joke.

"How did you get here, dear?" asked Edith.

"I came by cab. I cannot ride. My father will have a fit. He is overly protective. He forgets I'm almost eighteen."

"That's okay. We will take you back. You came to visit your grandparents, and that is okay."

Edith and Harold take her home. The children are delighted to see their Nana and Gramps. Phoebe is surprised but pleased. Madison admits she initiated the visit, and she is glad she did. Her grandparents are glad for the visit and in turn want to visit with their grandchildren.

Her father comes home shortly, surprised to see his parents and the children running and jumping on them. Madison tells him there is reason to celebrate. She is celebrating because she has a date. That sets him off on the dangers of dating. She turns to Phoebe. "You need to do something about him. He is out of control, Mom. I am serious," said Madison.

"Listen, daughter, I am not going to allow you to go out with just anyone. I must be comfortable with your date."

She turns her back and says softly to him, "You are worse than my mother. You fuss and are overprotective, and you hover. You should relax and trust your child."

He looks smug and says, "Did I tell you how very well I got along with your mother?"

"No need, Dad. I am the living proof of that," she says cheekily. His face turns red, and Madison laughs.

"Stepped in that one. Yes, set me up. Okay, think of that date and see if I let you go."

"Dad, don't you see? My memory is back!"

The others cheer and whoop. Maddi is back. Hip, hip hooray.

Epilogue

Madison calls her maternal grandparents, Ethel and Benjamin Brooks, and she apologizes and arranges a meeting. She invites Uncle Fitzroy and Aunt Carol's family. They have a breaking of bread to signal burying the hatchet. It is said they are stronger together than apart. Madison has both families talking. They plan to be in Mount Vernon for Thanksgiving. Uncle Fitz is thinking about settling down and will be getting married next year.

Auntie Jen and Madison have reconciled their differences. She has come to respect Madison. The pain of losing her mother is still there, but she is coping much better. She is close to her dad but finds him outrageous, and Phoebe remains her partial confidant and mother. She still has secrets locked away in her mother's journal for her eyes only.

Dr. Ridge is still interested in her. Their first date takes place at Manhattan B.B. King's Blues Club. They watch the legendary Eartha Kitt.

The End

About the Author

Claudette H. McLennon is a migrant from Jamaica who settled in New York for many years. She is an avid reader of romance novels, mysteries, and spy thrillers. She has an intimate and long-standing love affair with books. She loves the Bible stories as well as the Hardy Boys stories told her by her siblings. This sparked a love for writing stories. Hence, this story is the lively imagination of a teenager translated and brought to life forty years later.

This love of writing also led to publishing *Ode to Lillet Rose*, a book of poetry, and her first novel *Sins of the Parents* (due 2022). Currently retired, she is committed to writing more novels/ poetry. When not working as part-time Mary Kay consultant, she enjoys listening to music, doing crossword puzzles, doodling, arts and crafts, and light cooking.